The Lesbian Collection

Six Stories of Girl-on-Girl
Shrinking and Growing

By: Amber Collins

A Note . . .

While I love my husband very much, I loved women way before he came along. My first giantess fantasies came about when playing with my high school girlfriend. Back then, I was very shy about the whole idea, and it didn't help matters that she laughed at me when I said I'd love nothing more than to be her little shrunken sex toy— or for her to be mine.

I think women bring something special to this fantasy, especially when they enjoy it and don't consider it as simply a payday. I've met a few in this industry and if you're lucky enough to find the rare, actual girl who wants to shrink you down and make you hers . . . be good to her.

Below is a collection that celebrates the exclusivity of women. This fantasy, while primarily being male-centric, also caters to women. These fantasies are all mine, and have developed over the past several years. I hope you enjoy them as much as I enjoyed writing them.

Sorority
Sisters

"Wanna see something cool?" Jill asked, noticing Brie's head starting to bob and the magazine starting to slip from her fingertips.

"Yeah, I suppose," the woman said through a stifled yawn.

The girls were in the third-floor lab of St. Phillip University's science building. Last time Jill bothered to look at the wall clock it had been a few minutes past midnight. The custodians made a habit of locking all the labs at night—except this one. The other labs contained pricy equipment: computers, microscopes, SMART screens and other high-end electronics. The third-floor lab, the biology department HQ, housed mostly cages of small animals and long cabinets full of chemicals. Not things that would typically be stolen should someone decide to pop the door lock. In fact, the only machine in the lab was the nuclear centrifuge.

Jill and Brie had been asked to cowrite an article in a very prestigious medical journal on Dr. Parson's latest work. Dr. Parsons was SPU's own 'mad scientist' and had stumbled onto a rather unique formula originally intended to shrink cancer cells when injected into late-stage tumors. However, the formula worked a little too well.

And if that weren't enough, there was even a side-effect.

"Oh, is this the shrinking stuff?" Brie asked, jolting awake when she saw Jill pulling a blue case out of the mini-fridge.

"Indeed it is," she said, setting to work on making the formula viable. This was a lengthy process that took her roughly ten minutes now that she'd done it so many times. The binary ingredients had to be run through the nuclear centrifuge but not before she input data into the computer.

The formula could be controlled—and depending on what information she entered, the centrifuge would tailor the formula's composition in any way she saw fit. This allowed a remarkable number of variables to play with.

When she pulled the vial out of the centrifuge, still spinning, Brie noticed that it had taken on a turquoise, glowing hue. The stuff was pretty, like sparkling Gatorade.

"I didn't know it would be all glittery," said Brie, sliding it out while Jill picked up two guinea pigs and placed them in a rubber tote.

"It didn't use to be," said Jill. "Dr. Parsons changed a few things about it. She said it was too unstable and now when it's irradiated it glows. Scary stuff."

"So are we like . . . gonna get cancer from being around this thing?" Brie asked, swishing the contents of the vial back and forth.

Jill took it from her fingers, leaving the girl with a dumbfounded look. "There isn't nearly that much radiation. But don't swish it around. You don't want this stuff on you."

"Why not? Does it work on people?"

"Works on all living things, I would assume. But you have to drink it. I don't think it'll do much to your skin. But let's not take any chances." She pulled one of the guinea pigs out and said, "This is Robert and that's his girlfriend Emma."

Jill produced a medicine dropper and drew up a few drops of the glowing formula. She positioned both guinea pigs beneath her arm, first Robert and then Emma, and squeezed a tiny drop into each of their mouths. When she was finished, she returned the lid to the vial and watched the two guinea pigs with excited eyes.

Immediately, Robert darted across the tote and mounted Emma. The creatures made little adorable sounds while they fucked.

Brie put a hand to her face and laughed, feeling her cheeks turn red. "You've got to be kidding me."

"Nope. The formula makes stuff horny as hell. Everything we give it to wants to fuck."

Then, while the animals were still going at it, they began to dwindle away. Brie didn't know what was more intriguing, watching the animals have sex or watching them shrink before her eyes. Both creatures seemed oblivious that their world was getting larger, or perhaps they just didn't care. By the time they were finished, the guinea pigs were no bigger than mice. They fucked a few minutes longer, then separated and investigated their now much larger enclosure.

"Oh my God, that's awesome!" said Brie. "Dr. Parsons made a roofie drug that shrinks stuff!"

"I'm sure she didn't do it on purpose," said Jill, closing her laptop and packing her messenger bag.

"Bullshit. I always thought that lady would be a freak. You know, the good kind. I'm betting she made a sex drug and the shrinking is a side effect."

"You're ridiculous. Get the light, will you? I'm sleepy. Let's get home."

"So what will happen with the guinea pigs? They stuck like that forever?"

Jill shook her head. "No, I brewed it to wear off in twenty minutes."

"Interesting," said Brie.

"What is?"

"Nothing, just wondering how many times they'll fuck before they grow back."

Jill just rolled her eyes. "C'mon, dumbass."

***

Jill and Brie were inseparable—they were roommates, both worked at the Italian restaurant in town, and both had most classes together. They were even in the same sorority together. Most would even say they were lovers, but that wasn't true. They'd hooked up before, several times actually. But neither of them were relationship material for the other. It wasn't a priority. Both girls were young, at the peak of their lives, and wanted only to have fun.

"Sorority meeting tonight, did you know?" Brie asked, looking at her phone.

"Well we missed that one," said Jill, glancing up at the clock and seeing it was now almost one in the morning.

"They're going to kick us out," said Brie. "Well, you at least."

"They've never liked me," Jill said, settling down on the sofa and flipping on the television. Some infomercial selling gym equipment came on.

"It's not they, Jill. It's Megan."

Megan was the Queen B. The head honcho. The one who the Silver Sisters lived and died by. She was the one who ran the sorority and the one who kicked you out if you, say, missed meetings, didn't attend functions, or really contribute anything to the organization. Jill was looking to be cast out any day now.

"We are writing papers for Dr. Parsons's journal now. That'll look better on a resumé than a stupid sorority."

Brie shrugged as if it did not matter. She stood up, gave herself a stretch and said, "Try to be nice. Maybe if you had one thing to offer them, they'd be more favorable toward you." She cupped Jill's chin before walking off to her bedroom and shutting the door.

It was late and Jill was falling asleep but she wanted a shower before she went to bed. In the bathroom and after running water in the tub and dancing out of her jeans and t-shirt, she made a discovery. When her jeans hit the floor, she heard a metallic 'tink' on the tile. Digging in her pocket she came up with the vial of shrinking formula—while talking to Brie she'd absent-mindedly stowed it away.

She wouldn't get in trouble. Dr. Parsons had made gallons of the formula—it was easy and cheap to produce—the real magic came after the nuclear centrifuge had its way with it—so Jill wasn't too worried about this missing vial. Now, she was facing a new dilemma that she'd never considered until she was in the privacy of her own home with a sample of the formula.

She wanted to try it.

Uncapping the vial, she brought it up to her nose and gave it a sniff. There wasn't much of a smell, other than a faint sweet scent that reminded her of licorice. The glow was still there, but had faded slightly. That was normal. In about three hours the glow would dissipate completely but the formula would still work as intended.

But how safe was it for her? She'd seen it tested on creatures as large as a dog—Dr. Parsons gave a dose to her own German Sheppard—a male who tried to hump Jill's leg while it quickly shrank down to the size of a rabbit. Every test had been successful and each subject had responded just as intended.

So why not humans?

She wiped a hand across the steam on the mirror and looked at her reflection—a beautiful naked girl with long blond hair spilling down her chest. Without dwelling on it any further, she tipped the vial back, took a tiny, tasteless swig, then replaced the lid and put the vial on the sink counter. Her heart was thudding in her chest as she grabbed the marble and stared intently at herself, waiting for the change to occur.

It was taking a long time. She ventured to wonder if it even worked on humans. Maybe people were too big, or were too complex. Maybe it just took more time to spread throughout a human body.

That was what she was thinking when she suddenly felt a throbbing between her legs that almost brought her to her knees. She gripped the counter, her mouth agape. It felt like she'd just rammed her nine-inch vibrator right into her pussy. There'd never been a feeling like this. She was worried her teeth were going to shatter by the way she was shaking. A thin trickle of cum ran down her leg, mostly due to the surprise sense of euphoria.

The orgasm was enough to distract her from the feeling of her feet sliding across the tile. She was also doubling over a little, her head hanging as her body was wracked by pleasure, that she didn't notice the mirror was rising up, as was the sink basin. When the throes of the orgasm were almost over and she was left with a sense of immense pleasure, she snapped to her senses and noticed the room was expanding.

Now, her pleasure changed to panic as she didn't know how the formula was going to affect her. She didn't measure it so how was she to know if she'd overdosed or not? Sure, it was a small swig, but who knows how it would work in a human's body? She was stupid and rash to do this. But this pleasure . . .

She lay back against the tub, her fingers finding their way down to her wet pussy. Jill was amazed by how her feet pulled back away from the bottom of the sink. It couldn't have been more than a two-foot difference, too small for even a child to sit with legs extended, but here she was, a normally tall, lanky girl, now folding up like a telescope.

The back of the tub was cool as it rose above her head and she quickly stood, then hopped over the side, landing in waist-high warm water. When the warmness that had spread to all corners of her body subsided, she knew her shrinking had stopped. Jill trudged through the bath water and up to the faucet, now just above her head. If she had to guess, she was probably around two and a half feet tall, maybe a little less.

I'm shrunken, she thought. *The stuff actually worked. Brie's gonna flip out.*

The whole time she tried to take a bath, comical as it was, her mind kept drifting back to her roommate asleep just down the hall. Jill's fingers fumbled with the giant washcloth and she settled for using Brie's small bottle of body wash since her own bar of soap was on a shelf now much too high.

That big, sexy body . . .

Just down the hall . . .

She was probably only wearing panties. As hot as today had been, maybe not even those . . .

Jill danced out of the tub and used one of the hair towels to dry off. It amazed her to think that this once barely wrapped around her head and mess of blond locks. Now, it covered her whole body like a sheet.

She had to hop to reach the door's handle but luckily it was designed to be long and slender, so she needed only to grab it and pull. The door swung open, revealing the now cavernous hallway. Luckily they didn't own a cat or else this would be a treacherous trip. Her eyes had trouble focusing but that was because they were shrunken—she didn't see as far as she did before and they didn't take in as much light. Jill hurried down the hall, leaving tiny wet footprints behind her.

Brie's door was ajar, her air conditioner humming. When Jill entered she felt her nipples harden by the sudden cold air. It made a tiny coo escape her lips and her fingers found her sweet spot as she walked toward the bed that loomed above her head. Brie was asleep but turned over when the door opened. For a moment Jill caught sight of her foot hanging off the edge of the bed—it was simply massive—but it was quickly gone as the bed shifted then settled.

Currently, Jill didn't think she could climb the bed. Standing on her tiptoes, she still couldn't see onto it. If she ran and jumped she could perhaps grab handfuls of the sheet and lift herself up, but she may disturb Brie. She wanted to be quiet for now, so she settled on pulling out a shoebox from beneath the bed and standing on it.

There was Brie, in all her naked glory, lying on her back. Where Jill stood, the giantess's foot was obscuring most of what could be seen. It had been hot that day, and Brie was sweaty—something that made Jill's heart race. Not caring at the moment if she woke her friend or not, Jill leaned in, buried her face against Brie's sweaty sole and kissed. The woman was intoxicating—her scent was driving Jill wild and she felt a tingle between the legs. Jill even went so far as to wrap her arms around the foot and pull it toward her. Still, Brie barely moved.

But then she carried her foot away, knocking Jill off the box. The shrunken woman picked herself up and just laughed, but she wasn't laughing when she returned to her perch and saw her giant friend, legs now splayed open. Jill hoisted herself up onto the bed and crawled toward her friend's womanhood. It was so inviting . . .

Jill hoped she wouldn't wake Brie as she leaned in and ran her tongue along the giantess's lips. Brie tensed slightly, but then relaxed and Jill watched her sparse pubic hair stand on end. The tiny woman ventured to lick again, and the lick turned to a kiss and the kiss turned to a suck. Jill was on her knees now, arms stretched up to the lower part of Brie's stomach, her face buried in the giant pussy. Brie was getting wet, a smile upon her face. When the giant woman's fingers ran to her own hair, Jill knew she'd be waking up soon. With a stupor, the giantess's mouth opened followed by her eyes.

"What . . . the hell?" she asked, then the pussy was moving back so Brie could stand up. Jill just sat there on her knees, wiping her chin and smiling.

"Surprise?"

"Jill. Fuck, Jill. You *drank* that stuff?"

"Oh yeah, you bet your ass I did."

"Aren't you worried?" Brie asked. She was subconsciously closing herself off, drawing her knees up to her chest. "Do you feel okay?"

"I feel awesome. This has been an amazing experience."

"How long are you going to be like this?" Brie was rubbing the sleep from her eye, but Jill could tell she was relaxing a little.

Jill shrugged. "I don't know. I didn't measure it. I wasn't even sure how small I would get, although I must say, this is a pretty good size."

"You're so casual about all this. I'd be terrified."

"If you took some, you'd understand. It makes you so . . . *tingly*."

"I guess so," she said, reaching out and playing with Jill's hair. It was too much for the shrunken woman and she began kissing her friend's fingers.

Brie put her legs to either side of Jill and leaned in, kissing her tiny friend on the lips. It was the oddest experience. Brie did her best to stick her tongue in Jill's mouth but it wasn't happening. Likewise, Jill's tongue got lost along the vast lips of her giant friend.

"Mind letting me finish?" Jill asked, pointing between Brie's legs.

Brie rolled her eyes. "Fine, you little freak." She lay back, spread herself open.

Jill had just gotten back to work when she felt her body quiver. Brie's heartbeat pulsed around Jill's fingers since they were in the giantess's pussy up to the elbow. Then, it was getting tight and Jill had to get to her feet and wrench her arm free before it was stuck that way with definite consequences.

"Well, shit," said Jill, feeling her body spread across the bed. The formula was wearing off and she guessed it had been around twenty minutes since she'd drank it. She leaned in and did her best to massage Brie's clit with her mouth, and while the girl was arching her back and moaning, Jill couldn't help but feel some of the novelty was wearing off as she inched back to her regular size which, funny as it was, a head taller than Brie.

As the two normal-sized women lay in each other's arms and kissed, Jill couldn't help but realize she finally had something that would land her in Megan's favor. And she'd wanted to get in that woman's pants for some time— and the way into her pants might just be to have her shrink out of them.

***

Jill stopped by the sorority house the next morning to drop off paperwork she'd been skirting for two weeks. She was officially a member, had paid her dues, and was making sure that everything was fine. At this point, it would be really easy for Megan to rip up her recruitment form and hand back Jill's check. For some reason she didn't want that. She really didn't know why she desperately wanted to be a part of such an organization.

When the doors opened and she stepped into the foyer and saw no fewer than a dozen half-naked women causally strolling about, she remembered exactly why.

"Come to resign, I assume?" came the curt voice of Megan from her right. The Amazonian seductress came up to her and shook her head. "You know, we have girls on our waiting list who would love to be in here."

"I know, Megan, I know. I'm getting my paperwork squared away." She brought up the wad of paper that looked in no way professional or even legible. Jill wasn't an organized person and she sometimes forgot that people couldn't see the clarity she saw in her own mind.

"I'll just take that," said Megan, plucking it from her fingers. No sooner had she taken it that she wadded it up further, then tossed it onto the coffee table where a couple of girls—Madison and Hailey—were sitting cozied up. The lovers laughed at Jill's apparent dismissal from the sorority. "Leave. We don't need you, Jill."

"Wait, please," said Jill. "Come out with us tonight. Let's talk about it. Over drinks. On us."

"Us?" Megan said, her voice rising, just as Jill knew it would.

"Yeah, Brie and I want to take you out." Megan had a slight infatuation with Jill's roommate. "In fact, she was talking about that last night. I think she might be sweet on you, Meg."

Megan did her best to keep a stoic face but Jill knew better. The girl was soaking her panties right then and there. The tall woman walked back over to her, and Megan was one of the few women Jill had to look up to see. "Are you lying?"

"Lying? I'd never lie about this. You two would be cute together. I'm all for it."

Again, Megan did her best to keep composure but couldn't hold back the tiny grin from festering on her face.

"Okay. We'll see," said Megan, grabbing the wad of paperwork back from the table. "Cody's Shack?"

***

"I've never been there before," said Brie when Jill filled her in on what had happened. Cody's Shack was a bar across town that was popular with college students. However, with this being a Tuesday night, there probably wouldn't be many there.

"Me either, but I need you looking drop dead gorgeous," said Jill, laughing a little.

Brie rolled her eyes. "So you're pimping me out now? I guess I could do worse than Megan Hoosier."

"Exactly. So you be nice and I'll do the rest."

"The rest? What are you planning?"

Jill just smiled a little.

Brie shook her head and said, "No way. You're not thinking about shrinking her, are you?"

"Her. You. Me. It'll be fun."

"No way," said Brie. "I'm not taking any of that stuff."

"C'mon, take one dose with me and you'll see. You'll fucking love it, girl. Look at me. It didn't hurt me any."

"I don't know, Jill . . ."

"You know you want a monster orgasm. This'll give you one. Besides, being shrunken down is so cool."

Brie just stared at her for a moment. "Okay fine. I'll try it. But how are you going to get Megan to go along with it? I mean this is kind of scary and I've known the formula has existed for a while."

"You leave that to me," said Jill.

***

She spent the remainder of the morning in the lab mixing up a few vials of the formula. She wanted these to be different—slower acting, more powerful, and longer lasting. It was difficult math, but she spent a long time making sure her calculations were correct. Everything had to be perfect and some of the data she needed she was forced to guess. For example, she knew nothing of Megan's metabolism, nor her exact height and weight. Jill tailored a potion based on what she saw. No matter though. The formula gave lots of room for improvisation and she was fairly certain she'd get the desired results.

That night the three sat at the bar of Cody's Shack, drinking and talking about the most trivial things. While Megan might have been one of the sexiest women at the college, she certainly wasn't the smartest. Most of the topics Brie and Jill wanted to talk about were rewarded by a blank stare or at best, a confused laugh. So Jill stuck to the basics—clothes, pop culture, and sex.

They took a cab back to Brie and Jill's apartment. Megan lived in the sorority house which was just a walk down the road but the girls invited their leader up to talk. Megan, while a little tipsy, was in complete control and Jill couldn't help but notice how she stared at Brie's ass as it walked up the steps.

An hour later and the three were on the sofa, Megan sandwiched between them. They didn't talk long because Brie took the initiative and kissed the Amazonian woman full on the lips. Jill ran her fingers along the woman's jeans, then rubbed her crotch through the material. She was kissing the woman's neck when Megan laughed a little and started to fiddle with her buttons. Jill gave Brie the look and the make-out ground to a halt while they had Megan's full attention.

"We want to try something with you," said Jill, reaching into her purse. She pulled out three vials with the letters J, B, and M on their lids.

"You got Ecstasy? Never done it before, but okay, I guess," said Megan.

"No, not Ecstasy," said Jill. "Something better."

Megan sat up, sobered. "What is it then?"

"Let's say we could give you the best orgasm you've ever had . . .," started Brie. "But, you kinda have to shrink while it's happening."

"Wait . . . what?" asked Megan.

Jill said, "Dr. Parsons came up with a shrinking formula." She held up the vial with the M on it. "This will make you shrink down to about six inches but while it's happening, you'll feel like your skin is electrified. Your pussy will throb like it's never throbbed."

"Is this some kind of joke? What are you going to do, give me something to knock me out then take a bunch of photos?"

"No, Megan, we promise," said Brie. "We're gonna take one too. It's gonna be fun. We'll shrink and fuck and get off and then fuck again when we're small. Right, Jill?"

"Sounds like a plan to me," said Jill.

"I've never taken it, but Jill woke me up last night while she was shrunk. This tiny bitch was eating me out like there was no tomorrow."

"For real?" She turned to Jill for confirmation.

"Go ahead and drink it," said Jill, handing her the bottle. She started pulling Megan's jeans down. "I'll do the same for you too."

Megan looked at the vial. Said, "and it's safe?"

"Of course it's safe. Brie just told you I've used it before."

Jill started to kiss her panties and could already tell from Megan's scent that the woman was probably drenched. Feeling the woman's lips so close to her pussy, separated by only a lacy pair of panties made Megan tip the bottle back and drain it. Brie and Jill did likewise.

This was going to be fun.

Jill could feel Megan's body melting away, as the Queen B's potion was brewed to work faster than her own. Jill pulled the panties aside and slid two fingers inside the dwindling woman, eliciting a moan and an arching of the back. Megan's own fingers were in Jill's hair, contracting, inching shorter, stubbier. Brie helped her out of the quickly loosening clothes and finally Jill nearly pulled the woman into the floor when the panties were yanked away. All three laughed and looked around, noticing how the world was changing.

"Why am I so much smaller than the two of you?" Megan asked, looking up at Jill's large eyes as the woman licked her pussy in long, slow strides. It was true. Although Jill and Brie were nearing the halfway point, Megan was much smaller, almost the size of a Barbie doll when she posed the question. Brie just shook her head, genuinely not knowing the answer.

"Because it's your first time and I want to be a little bigger than you," said Jill. "You won't mind."

And of course, she didn't.

The girls continued to shrink until Megan had reached a size of six inches tall. Both Jill and Brie fought their way out of their oversized, skimpy outfits and stood at an even foot tall. All three were in the floor by the sofa, surrounded by giant panties and shoes and the empty vials. Megan looked up at the two amazons, relatively speaking, and licked her lips. She put a hand up to Brie's thigh, to which the woman just leaned into it. Jill could still taste Megan on her lips.

"We've got an hour to play," said Jill, dropping down to her knees. She slipped Megan's nipple into her mouth while Brie moved forward, burying the half-sized woman's face right into her pussy. Megan could barely lick, so lost was she to the euphoria. Jill grinned as she looked into the shrunken woman's eyes. This was a great idea, and before long she'd have the Queen B eating out of her hand.

It was nice seeing just how much Brie liked the potion. Just as Jill had learned before, it caused one of the best orgasms possible. Her friend was more vocal than she could ever remember, taking turns between riding the half-sized Megan's face, and simply lying back and letting her friends work her over. Jill had always been so attracted to her, but now, at such a small size with the induced orgasm always looming nearby, it was an experience that made normal sex seem dull.

Megan was enjoying being a shrunken fucktoy. Jill and Brie both took turns working her over, moving from one end to the other. Jill, with a proclivity for feet, sucked the woman's shrunken toes and licked along her soles, gingerly moving lips up north. After the hour was up, Jill couldn't believe the tiny woman could possibly cum anymore. Then again, how could any of them? The floor was slick from their juices.

Megan's potion wore off first, her tiny body spasming before inching bigger. It was a turn on for Jill, who'd been between her legs when the change began, and could feel Megan's growing pussy beneath her tongue. When the woman was double Jill and Brie, their potions wore off and now all three were closing the distance to their normal sizes. Megan climbed upon the sofa and sat there, mesmerized to watch her feet grow past the cushion, her legs bend at the knees and drop to the floor as she slid into her final height.

"Thoughts?" Jill asked just before her growth stopped. Brie threw herself into the armchair next to the sofa and was breathing heavily, but smiling nonetheless.

Megan just looked back and forth at the two girls, as if in some sort of drunken stupor. She ran a finger through her hair and laughed. She raised her arms above her head and shrugged. "Definitely an experience," she purred. "But a good one."

"Would you be willing to do it again?" asked Brie, raising a seductive eyebrow that Jill knew was sincere.

Megan looked at Jill for a moment, then down to her naked lap, as if reminiscing on what just happened there. "Most definitely."

Each of the girls showered in turn as the night went on. Megan was first, then Brie second. While Jill waited her turn and Megan sat on the sofa, pulling her panties up, the two managed a quick conversation.

"So I think she really likes you," said Jill.

Megan glanced down toward the bathroom, listening to the water steam. "You think so?"

"Definitely."

"And what about you?" she asked.

"Me?" Jill was taken aback.

"Yes, you." Megan pulled her shirt on and crossed her legs.

"I most definitely do," Jill said. Although she was attracted to Megan, she didn't like her nearly as much as her friend. However, if this secured a spot with the Silver Sisters, why not exaggerate a little?

Megan moved over to sit next to Jill, running a finger along the beauty's bare leg. "Got any more of the stuff?"

"Not with me. But I can get all you want." Jill leaned in and planted a kiss. Megan's lips barely moved. Either she wasn't into the kiss or that tidbit of information caught her off guard.

Megan leaned back, stared at her for a moment as though sizing her up. At last, she said, "How would you like to be an officer?"

"Me? An officer?"

Megan nodded. "I've been wanting to shake things up in the sorority. I think you could help make that possible. But tell me more about the stuff."

By the time Brie had finished her shower, Jill had explained to Megan all about Doctor Parsons's work. About the shrinking formula and the interesting side-effects. Jill explained how easy it was to make, that after a bit of difficult math she could tailor the potions to be wildly versatile. Megan seemed to cross her legs tighter at the mention of this.

When Brie entered the room, still wearing a towel, Megan stood and said she needed to be getting home.

"When is the next meeting?" Jill asked, determined not to miss it.

"Next Friday," said Megan. "I really hope you both come. I didn't appreciate that you missed the last one."

Jill shrugged. "Maybe we were there. But we were so small that you didn't see us."

Megan raised a seductive eyebrow, the gears in her head turning. She was going to capitalize on the potions, and Jill would probably let her.

***

The next day Jill received a text from Megan that included a laundry list of requests. She wanted potions—lots of potions. Megan had requested at least three that were very specific—detailing sizes, durations, and rates of shrinking and wanted to know if it were all possible. Jill wasn't so sure she could get them made by the time of the meeting but messaged Megan back and told her it wouldn't be a problem at all. Megan simply replied with a 'thumbs up' emoji that made Jill roll her eyes. How she hated that thing.

It was difficult but Jill cut classes for two days to work tirelessly in the lab. Doctor Parsons's current setup wasn't meant to mass-produce shrinking potions, so Jill did her best to mix the ingredients and then line them up to be irradiated. It was a slow process, producing only two or three an hour once she'd mixed them up. The hardest part was doing the math, and although she excelled in such things, it was a complicated formula to figure out a specific size, duration, and rate—like predicting the path of astral bodies. When she was finished, she kept them all in a portable cooler.

Friday night came and Jill and Brie arrived early. There were a few Silver Sisters already there, already drinking, and already scowling in Jill's general direction. Brats Hailey and Madison were among the worst. The sorority house was a large building but most of the girls hung out in the common room in front of the massive television that Megan procured through a successful, albeit shady, fundraiser. When Megan appeared on the upstairs landing, she held her hands up and said, "My newest officers, welcome!"

This caused a hush to fall across the room, for officer was a rank that was earned through works— something none of them had seen performed by Jill. She made a mock bow, then held up the cooler for Megan to see, to which the Queen B threw her head back and laughed. "Now we're gonna have some fun!" she said, coming down to the common room.

The girls handed off the cooler and then started to drink and mingle. Most of the Silver Sisters were rude or downright hostile, but that was okay. Some were even overly friendly, knowing that the best way to get into Megan's good graces was to accept her new favorites as one of their own. As the night grew dark and the meeting commenced, Jill and Brie found themselves on a sofa across from three other Silver Sisters: Kara, Dianne, and Stephanie. Each of them was vying for the spot of officer. And each of them looked at Jill and Brie with hate-filled eyes, knowing that the two girls simply happened upon the opportunity by unknown means.

Megan appeared in front of the television holding a cardboard box that Jill noticed contained at least three of the potions. Jill had labeled the sides with a sticky note, indicating what each one did. Also in the box was a large, foam cube but Megan came around and sat on the edge of the coffee table, blocking their view.

She was wearing thick combat boots, baggy jeans, and a tight-fitted t-shirt. Her hair was pinned back and she had a wide grin upon her face. When she seated herself, the whole house went to a whisper. Her hands were clasped across her knees and she surveyed the room. The three officer hopefuls sat up straight, as if the illusion of appearing taller would make them more desirable to Megan's eyes.

"You all have met our newest officers, Jill and Brie," said Megan, outstretching her hand.

"How is this possible, Meg?" asked a dark-skinned girl from the doorway. "We didn't vote. You just let them rank up?"

"That I did, Sarah. I won't explain myself." Megan furrowed her brow in anticipation of resistance but there was none. The girl named Sarah simply shook her head and leaned against the doorway.

"These girls earned it," said Megan. "And we have room for one more officer." She turned to look at the trio of perfectly placed Silver Sisters. "One of you has a shot."

"Just tell us what we need to do," said Kara, her voice soft yet resolute.

"First, I need a volunteer." She didn't even notice all the hands that shot up as she turned back to the box and pulled from it one of the vials. She uncorked it, handed it to the nearest Silver Sister, a tall, red-headed girl.

"Drink it," said Megan.

"What is it?" asked the girl.

Megan shook her head then took the vial back. "Sit." Then, to the room, "I need another volunteer." More hands went up, although more hesitantly. She approached a girl seated on the sofa across from the three officer hopefuls, a lithe, raven-haired girl with dark skin. This one eagerly took the potion without question and drank it in one gulp, then tossed the potion aside.

No one knew what to expect but by the way Megan so intently watched her, everyone in the room assumed *something* would be happening. The girl fanned herself and drew her legs up, then looked around embarrassed. What no one knew (other than her and the three with experience) was that she was building toward a massive orgasm. It became tough for her to keep it out of her face and just when Jill was sure she'd make a cry of ecstasy, that's when her body began to change. A chorus of cries went up as the girl began to dwindle away, her clothes loosening, her shoes dropping to the floor. She tried to stand but tripped over her own skirt, to which Megan laughed riotously and stooped down to help her up.

By the time Megan placed her on the sofa the girl had shrunken down to three-feet tall, then suddenly stopped. The test-subject looked around, noticing the giant ladies closing in to gawk. It was probably terrifying but Jill couldn't feel sorry for her. It was a great orgasm—easily noted by the stream of cum trailing down the shrunken woman's leg—and it was also harmless. She would grow back in twenty minutes.

"Change me back!" the little woman said, covering herself with her oversized shirt.

"Calm down, you'll be big again soon," said Megan. "Thank me later for the orgasm." The shrunken woman's face turned red and she looked down to her lap.

"I just wanted you all to see this before I begin," said Megan. "I wanted you to know that shrinking technology exists, and if you three plan on becoming an officer, you're going to have to shrink." They looked at one another, then eventually gave weak nods.

"Okay," said Stephanie. "Give it to me. I'll do it."

Megan laughed and pulled the box onto her lap. "I'm afraid it isn't that easy."

Stephanie pulled her hand back, as if slapped on the wrist.

Megan pulled out the large foam cube and for the first time Jill could see that she'd written words on each side with a black marker. Megan tossed it up into the air, but Jill only caught the words "BRA" and "PANTIES" before the Queen B steadied it between her knees.

"We're going to play a little game," said Megan. "You three are going to please your queen. You each will roll the die, and wherever it lands, that's where you'll go." Megan leaned back, then waved a hand across her own body. "Who's first?"

"I'll do it," said Stephanie, taking the cube. She tossed it up into the air. It came down, bounced once on the table and landed on the floor. "BRA" was face-up.

Megan jiggled her own breast and said, "I expect you to suck my nipple while you're in there." Stephanie's eyes grew at the thought, probably realizing just how small she'd need to be. All the while, Megan was fishing out the correct potion. Jill had wondered why she'd wanted specific sizes and this was clearly the reason. Stephanie took the bottle, then drained it.

"Get undressed, girl," Megan commanded. "I want to feel skin on my skin."

Stephanie nodded and handed the vial back to Megan. She was already feeling the effects of the orgasm as she slipped out of her dress. The other two hopefuls exchanged nervous glances but couldn't tear their eyes from the dwindling woman. Stephanie didn't care that her own fingers found her sweet spot and began doing circles as she grew smaller, finally disappearing behind the coffee table. Megan leaned down, fished through the pile of clothes and produced the shrunken woman on the palm of her hand, now only three inches tall. "Don't let me down," Megan said to the girl, just before pulling her shirt out and dumping the shrunken woman inside.

Megan did a little dance, pulling at her shirt and bra, aligning the shrunken woman and putting her in a comfortable position. "Next?" she said, holding out the die for either Kara or Dianne to take. Dianne was the first to snatch it, then tossed it into the air, letting it land on the sofa between them. It read "PANTIES" across the top. Dianne just looked up at her, a mix of horror and intrigue.

Megan held out the next potion and said, "I hope you're as energetic as Stephanie. Bonus points if you go inside my pussy. Not just clit stuff, okay?" Dianne didn't say a word, only looked pale as she slowly tilted the potion back and drank.

The color came back to her face as the first waves of pleasure washed over her. She tossed aside as much as dropped the vial as the orgasm came and she crossed her legs tightly. Megan helped undress the dwindling girl, pulling her shoes and socks off. Dianne's feet quickly disappeared into the legs of her jeans before those too came off. Everyone was amazed to watch the shrinking as this time it happened on the sofa—all eyes stayed with Dianne as the girl grew smaller and smaller until she stopped, also at three inches tall.

Megan scooped her up and then sat on the sofa. She unzipped her pants and placed Dianne on her stomach. The shrunken woman looked up at the giant woman and Megan gave her a confused, irritated look. "Why you looking at me, girl? Pussy is the other way." Megan slid a thumb under the hem of her panties and lifted them. Dianne turned around, got down on hands and knees, then disappeared beneath the line of fabric. Megan looked the room over and grasped the edge of the sofa, biting her lip. "Oh, she's wasting no time. She went right in."

"My turn," Kara said, asking as much as telling.

"Indeed, girl," said Megan. "You might get my other tit. Or maybe you can fuck Dianne inside me. That would be so fucking hot. C'mon, roll."

Kara tossed the die and it landed on the table. It read "SOCK."

Kara looked confused as Megan reached into the box and pulled out another vial. "I've had these combat boots on all day. Gonna be funky." Megan started unlacing her boot, then slid her foot out. Jill could smell just how sweaty it was and she was sitting almost five feet away.

Kara gulped and started to drink the potion before Megan stopped her and said, "Take your clothes off now. This one is gonna make you really small and we might have trouble finding you." Again, the girl went white as a ghost but she listened and did as she was told. Megan got down between her legs and started licking along her thighs as the woman quaffed the potion. Jill and Brie both found it arousing to watch the beauty shrink away, whilst being eaten out, whilst the perpetrator had two shrunken women pleasing *her*. By the time Kara's shrinking had stopped, she was absolutely minuscule—now only half an inch tall.

Megan seated herself on the sofa again and pulled off her sock, then crinkled her toes. She bunched up the fabric, brought it to the edge of the sofa and told Kara, "Jump in, little lady." Kara looked up at her, then back down into the void of the strong-smelling fabric. Jill through the little girl was backing out, but Megan brought a finger up behind the tiny person and pushed her right in. It was possible she screamed, but it was too low to hear. Megan gingerly pushed her foot back in, moving her toes so that the tiny woman was pinned between her big toe and the one next to it, then put the boot back on.

"I can't even feel her in there," said Megan. "But the other two girls are earning their spot for sure." Megan lay back and let the shrunken people please her. After a moment, while everyone was looking at her, she pointed to the box and said, "Have at them. Shrink, fuck, enjoy. You won't be sorry."

By the time the first four girls who'd been shrunken tonight were due to become normal sized again, half the room had started to experiment with shrinking. Jill and Brie both took a potion and found a corner for themselves until a couple of larger girls decided to join in, loving using fingers like dildos. Jill came all over a girl's hand as the giantess let her ride. Brie did likewise, wishing she were small enough to be dildo-sized like Dianne had been earlier.

Megan started to prepare for the girls' re-enlargement. She stripped down to nothing and watched as Stephanie grew back across her chest, still sucking as the woman slid to the side, beautiful hair spilling all across

Megan. She could feel when Dianne started to grow back and allowed the woman to stay inside her until she'd become around eight inches, then it became too painful and the shrunken woman had to be pulled out. She was covered in Megan's juices, her hair a matted mess.

Kara, who'd only been stuck to Megan's sole by sweat began to enlarge, dropping down to her heel and coughing. She didn't seem particularly pleased but smiled up at the woman nonetheless. When she was full-sized, she bounded off to take a shower, but quickly returned to the size-enhanced orgy.

Later in the night, Megan sat drinking a tall glass of wine, thinking if she were half-sized she'd have double the drink. Jill came and sat down next to her and said, "So who is your newest officer?"

Megan giggled. "All of them. How could I turn them away after all that?"

"You're becoming nice now?" said Jill.

Megan shrugged. "I'm not always the Queen B. I can respect my girls when it's deserved. And I really respect you. You've given us something that we'll be enjoying for a long time."

"Who knows where this technology will go in the future?" Jill asked.

"What do you mean?" Megan wondered.

"Doctor Parsons has done a lot with it. She wants to make it more customizable. Imagine being able to grow just your breasts or your lips or your hair."

"That would be handy," said Megan, taking a long swig from her glass.

"And one day, she hopes to make things grow. That's what I'm excited about."

"Would be fun to rip through clothes and tower over everyone," said Megan, lost to that thought. "So what now?"

"What now?" Jill asked.

"With us, with Brie. What now?"

Jill reached into her purse and pulled out two things. One was a potion vial and the other was a clear dildo. She unscrewed the end of the dildo, revealing that it was hollow enough to put something inside it. Megan's mind made the connection and her face went red. Jill looked over to the crowd of women, most shrunken, almost all engaged in some sort of sexual fun. Brie was currently naked, holding a glass of wine, while a half-sized woman's face was buried between her legs.

Jill held the vial up to Megan and smiled. "Drink up and get in there." Then she motioned toward Brie and added, "and I'll make sure you get in *there*."

The Fairy
in the Woods

Katherine's skin was sticky in the afternoon sun. The forest was thinning around her current spot and she walked faster to get to the thickening copse of trees just ahead. She'd been in this forest for three hours now, her little red, rusty Pontiac sitting on the side of the road several miles back. It was a lucky turn of events that she was able to take this assignment for extra credit in her biology class. Naturally, she loved being outdoors, in the woods, away from the hustle and bustle of the city. And given the task of cataloging plants for her end of semester project made it all the better.

She stopped to rest for a moment, pulling her backpack off and then kneeling down in the grass under the shade of a large oak tree. Her canteen was nearly empty but she'd brought along her water purification tablets and the sounds of a river were never far from her ears. This tract of forest was surrounded by city—one of the last spots of true nature to be found for about a hundred miles. Why even now, if she stood upon a tall enough hill, she could see the banking building of her town, in the far-off distance.

By the time the sun was the highest in the sky, she was running out of water and needed a break. With little effort she found the stream, a bright, bubbling current that sprayed coolness against her skin. Katherine pulled off her boots and sweaty socks and then dipped her feet in the cold water, instantly feeling revitalized. She dropped a couple of water purification tabs into her canteen, shook them around, and took a long, heavy drink. It was so tranquil here—no sounds of vehicles, construction, or people screaming into cellphones—the staples of the city. She could live here forever . . .

Later, she came to an oak tree with a base as big as her car. It looked ancient, weathered and cracked. The thick branches of the base curved up to create a halo of leaves along the top half of the monstrously large tree. Little animals scurried about, squirrels that could hide in the wrinkly bark and then scamper off again. For some reason Katherine was drawn to this tree, which sat in the middle of a clearing of grass so short it looked as though the forest employed a gardener. But that was impossible, way out here.

She found herself growing very tired so she decided to rest at the base of the giant tree. Whenever the wind blew, it was as though voices carried on it, and she looked over her shoulder more than once, sure there would be someone watching. As weird as this notion was, she felt no fear, no anxiety. In fact, it was as though she were drawn to the idea of voices, to the fact that others could be in the forest with her.

As she settled against the tree (which was far more comfortable than she would've guessed ancient, gnarled bark would feel) she began to think of her college roommate Cheryl. Perhaps it was the wind-stirred-voices that reminded her of the lady's smooth, sultry tone. Or maybe something in the water and air and earth had made her start to feel . . . tingly. She and Cheryl lacked any sort of romance but they sure made up for it in physical encounters. She slept in Cheryl's bed more often than her own, and in those quiet moments, both women would be lost to a euphoria that neither had experienced before.

Katherine's tanned legs went limp as she unfastened her belt and unbuttoned her shorts. Gingerly, her fingers slid across her stomach, over the rough patch of stubble and onto her sweet spot. She let her head touch the tree—which felt surprisingly soft, almost like a pillow—and then her fingers were working as best they could. Katherine's mouth opened as a tiny moan escaped her lips. One hand was in her hair, on her face, pulling at her own collar. Her toes were scrunching up in the boots.

When her muscles tightened and she knew the orgasm was right around the corner, a bug flew right toward her face and she was forced to swat it away, nearly losing her momentum. The tingle left her pussy for just a moment but quickly returned when her fingers got back on track. Twice more the irritating bug buzzed her and twice more she had to slow down and move to the side. Finally, when the orgasm was at its crescendo, she uttered a tiny cry and then collapsed, but not before noticing something on her knee.

Sitting on her bottom was a tiny woman, head thrown back in ecstasy because she was imitating exactly what Katherine had been doing moments before. The little woman had blond hair with wings to match, currently folded along her back so she could sit with her legs extended. She wore a green tunic that looked like silk with leggings that disappeared in brown, pointed boots. Her hand was shoved down the front of her pants, fingers bringing a tiny squeal to the girl. Katherine's first instinct was the swat her away but she couldn't help but watch. There was literally a fairy about to cum on her knee.

When the tiny thing's orgasm ripped through her delicate body, she let out a scream that was both adorable and a turn on. Katherine couldn't explain it other than perhaps she was still worked up from fingering herself. This little woman's body relaxed, or at least Katherine thought so. She was surprisingly light, as if there was nothing perched there at all. When the orgasm came to a close and the fairy withdrew her hand, she looked up and found the giant eyes of her observer. Katherine didn't know what to do other than smile.

"Hi," the fairy said, waving a hand of beautifully manicured fingers. Her nails were green to match her clothes. Did fairies have nail techs? This whole thing was preposterous but Katherine couldn't help getting caught up in it.

"Um, hi," Katherine returned. "So . . . that was fun, yeah?"

"Totally fun." The little fairy's cheeks flushed a bright red but she didn't look away. "I wanted to help but didn't know how. So I just joined."

"Help? What do you mean?" Katherine asked.

The fairy stood up on Katherine's knee and walked to the edge, arms behind her back. She looked over, which was quite a drop considering the little woman stood at around six inches. It took a moment to follow her eyes, which were aimed right at Katherine's unzipped crotch and flowery panties poking through.

"Oh," Katherine said, catching her meaning.

"I've never seen a big person up close," said the fairy, taking to flight. Her little wings tousled Katherine's hair as she hovered close. "My name is Liara."

"I'm Katherine." The fairy held out her hand to which Katherine delicately took it between her thumb and forefinger and gave it a tiny shake. The little woman was gorgeous up close, even though Katherine had trouble making out the features on a face so small, like looking at a highly-detailed doll with bad eyes. If she had to guess, Katherine assumed Liara was about her age.

"I didn't know fairies were real," said Katherine.

The little woman glowered. "You can't say fairy. That's *our* word. You can call me a Tree Nymph."

"Oh," said Katherine, embarrassed. "Okay. I'll remember that."

Liara burst into laughed, the weight of it spinning her around in midair. She returned, put a hand on Katherine's cheek and said, "I'm only kidding. Fairy, Liara. Whatever you want to call me."

"Good to know. I'm still unsure how you're real."

"There's plenty of us. All girls."

"That doesn't make sense," said Katherine. "How do you, you know? Procreate?"

"Uh, we come out of the roots, duh!" She said this as if it should be obvious.

"The roots?"

"Yes, the roots. Fairies are not of this world. We are the protectors of the forest and there have always been twelve of us. If one of us dies, the tree sends another to take our place. It's how it's been done for a thousand years."

"No boys?"

"No boys."

"But you seem to enjoy sex. Or getting yourself off, at least," said Katherine, feeling another tingle between her legs.

"I love the female body, mine included. We aren't so different," said the fairy, doing a little twirl and then landing on Katherine's knee.

"Except you have wings and I'm a giantess compared to you."

"Both can be temporarily altered, actually."

"How so?" asked Katherine.

She turned around, struck a pose and placed a hand upon her ass. Katherine wondered what kind of seduction she was attempting but realized it was to show how her wings simply fell off like water but instantly turned to dandelions that blew away in the wind. Now, she simply looked like a shrunken woman, albeit a shrunken woman with slightly pointed ears.

"Would you like to come see our tree?" said Liara. At first Katherine didn't catch her meaning but then it became clear.

"You mean . . . *inside* the tree?"

The fairy nodded.

"I . . . I don't know. Sounds kinda scary."

Liara rolled her eyes, and an instant later the wings were back, popping into place as if they'd never left. Little feet leaped from Katherine's knee and moved the fairy up to her ear, the wind moving aside her hair.

"We could fuck . . .," the fairy whispered, returning to Katherine's knee. She looked up at the giant woman and smiled innocently.

"I . . . I don't know. How would that even work?"

"It would work very well. Just gotta shrink you first."

"How?" asked Katherine, starting to feel onboard.

"With fairy magic, of course. Do you want to try it?"

"Can you change me back?" asked Katherine.

The fairy giggled and said, "Of course I can! I want to play with a big person too!"

"Okay. I guess we can do that."

"Wonderful!" the fairy said, lifting off and hovering in the air just above Katherine's head. "Okay, bear with me. I've never done this before." She outstretched her arms and a soft, tranquil light filled her hands. Liara dropped her head to her chest and her lips began to utter a quiet spell. Katherine's heart was beating fast, unsure how to feel at that moment. Was she really about to be shrunken down to fairy size?

Liara's spell came to an end and she opened her eyes and looked up. At the same time the soft glow left her fingertips and surrounded Katherine with what felt like little eyelashes. Her entire body was encased in the golden light, and in that moment she felt a twinge in her stomach and a stirring further down, the anticipation of what was going to happen next. When the light faded, Katherine looked around, but nothing had changed.

But then her ass was sliding across the forest floor, her panties becoming loose, followed by her shirt. Liara landed on the ground between her legs but she looked different—mainly because as the seconds slipped away, the tiny girl became larger. Or, more appropriately, Katherine was shrinking.

Her back rubbed against the bark as she made her descent toward the ground. Her feet shrank from the boots, leaving the socks hanging halfway out. The forest grew around her, rocks doubling in size, leaves stretching out to be blankets. Liara was standing a few feet away, beautiful, smiling face coming into focus as Katherine quickly shrank into her panties. The shirt collapsed above and after a moment of tunneling her way out, she got her bearings.

That ancient oak now looked gargantuan, the foliage above her impossibly far. A shadow fell over Katherine as she was looking up, and then she heard a voice above say, "Oops."

When she turned around, expecting to see a fairy of the same size, she was quickly drawn to the massive pair of leather boots in front of her. Katherine craned her head up to see the giant fairy standing over her, looking down with confused eyes and hands over mouth. This is how Katherine must have appeared to Liara moments ago, because their sizes had effectively switched.

"I'm so, so sorry!" said Liara.

"What the hell happened?" demanded Katherine.

"I used too much magic!"

"Well fix me, dammit!"

"Well . . ." The fairy, who looked anything but dainty right now, glanced up at the tree. "Not so simple for me."

Katherine was furious. "What? You're saying I'm stuck this way?"

"No, no!" Liara said, getting down on her knees. "My mother. She can fix you."

"I sure hope so," Katherine said, voice lowering. "Can we go see her?" She was suddenly not liking the feeling of being so small.

"I'm sorry, I didn't mean to scare you," said Liara. She bent down, picked up the tiny woman in her hand and then sat against the tree. "Can I calm you down?"

She opened her hand and Katherine was sitting on her palm, staring up at the most beautiful face she'd ever seen. The smile, the way she bit her lip—all so enticing.

"Okay," said the shrunken woman.

"Now don't get upset with me again, okay? But I want to try something I think you'll like."

"Okay," Katherine repeated.

Then, without warning, the fairy used one hand to pull out the hem of her leggings and the other to dump Katherine right in. Immediately the shrunken, naked woman felt a tingle between her legs because the giantess-fairy was so wet and so sticky. Her scent threatened to drive Katherine wild. The tiny woman flipped so that she stood against the fairy's pussy lips, happy that the otherworldly creature had matching anatomy.

"Go inside me," said Liara somewhere above her. Katherine did as she was told, using the fingers to pull the giantess apart and then slip first a leg in, and then the rest of her body. The fairy quivered by the tiny woman's movements and the transition to the inside was met with warmth and wetness. Katherine ran a hand across the pussy walls then licked her fingers, loving the girl's scent and taste. It was a tight fit, but whenever Liara relaxed, she was given more room to move about. At a relative six inches, she was able to slip so far in that her head was beyond the lips. Now, it was full darkness.

Katherine could feel the giantess writhe about as she kicked her legs. When the cave became even hotter, and even wetter, she knew she was doing a good job. The heartbeat of the fairy could be felt with each tightening of the pussy walls. Eventually the movement became so erratic that Katherine felt she was no longer in control of the woman's pleasure, and instead of kicking about simply grabbed nearby flesh and held on. A moment later she was drenched as a torrential flood washed over her, accompanied by the orgasmic cries of the woman on the other side of the pussy.

Light flooded the sanctuary and fingers grasped Katherine beneath the arms and pulled her out. The woman held her up and the next thing she knew, she was swimming in Liara's mouth. The giantess was sucking the juices off her shrunken body and Katherine couldn't help but reach fingers below and play with her own pussy, to which Liara sensed and used a tongue to help.

When the tiny woman was spent, she was pulled out and placed gently on the ground between the fairy's legs. Liara had been good enough to place a leaf beneath her, so that the dirt wouldn't cling to her sweaty skin.

"Are you calm?" asked the fairy.

Katherine nodded. "Very much so. That was wonderful."

"It was," said Liara, looking aloof. Then she brought herself back to her senses and said, "C'mon. I'll take you to my mother. But I want to hide you. It's kind of embarrassing that I shrunk you too much."

Katherine nodded and the fairy stood up with her, then placed her gently on the inside of the silk tunic. Liara's skin smelled divine as she rested against the giantess's breast. From here she could feel the heartbeat, and the heat emanating off the fairy's skin.

The next moment Katherine was clinging to the girl's breast even harder because the fairy had taken to flight. Straight up they soared, a moment in the blinding light of the midday and the next in darkness as Liara moved into the tree. It smelled so good here—like baking bread, but that was impossible. Then again, what about today had been logical? Ever since she'd stopped at the tree to rest, things had gone from sane to crazy.

Next they were on solid ground, Liara's footsteps jarring her. Katherine couldn't help but reach up, take the fairy's nipple in her hand and squeeze it, then after pulling herself closer, slipping it into her mouth. It was too big to fit, especially after it hardened and got longer with the fairy's arousal.

Katherine heard voices—more than a couple—as Liara carried her by. She dared a peek through the fairy's button hole, and spied several other girls, all large, all with parted wings that they kept down low. Their hair was often motley-colored, Liara's being the plainest of all. Each girl was beautiful but Liara held some sort of flair that they didn't possess. Still, it was arousing being so small in the proximity of so many luscious creatures.

Liara carried her up a flight of steps that twisted and turned so far that Katherine wondered just how far into the top of tree they would venture. Then again, both were very small, so the distance probably wasn't so far away. At the top the light was streaming in through oval windows that had been carved just below where the foliage started. When the wind would blow, Katherine could see giant-sized leaves bending down to cover the portals for a moment. Liara pulled her out and placed her on a bed, then got down on her knees to address the tiny woman.

"That's my mother's room," she said, pointing across the massive chamber to a wide door decorated with carvings that Katherine couldn't believe were possibly done by hand. "Let me go talk to her first. Humans and fairies aren't supposed to mix."

"God, I'm gonna be stuck this way, aren't I?" Katherine pouted, thinking of how ridiculous she must look standing there, naked and only a fraction of an inch tall.

"Calm down, it'll be fine. Just let me talk to her." With that, the fairy bounded across the room and through the door, leaving Katherine there on the bed alone.

She couldn't jump in the floor from this height so she moved around the bed, admiring the woodwork. The fairies had taken great strides to decorate this place. Liara's room looked much like the one Katherine had back in college and before that, at home. It was brightly adorned, smelled wonderful, held a bookshelf, a table, a couple of chairs and the big fluffy bed in which Katherine found herself walking. There was a pair of gigantic shoes sitting on the edge that had the sweet, sticky scent of the giantess's feet inside.

A moment later Liara returned, dropped to her knees to let Katherine walk across the bed and hop onto her outstretched hand. "See? Nothing to worry about. Mother will fix you right up."

She carried her through the door to an equally ornate room. This one had a vaulted ceiling with a hanging, wooden chandelier. Little lights hung atop the candles—celestial to the point of being supernatural. Real fire didn't come in such hues, and real fire didn't play by such rules in the confines of woodwork. Liara placed her atop a dresser and Katherine's eyes were immediately drawn to the regal woman standing by the bed.

She was older than Liara but it didn't look so. The fairy genes were good because the mother of Liara had blond hair like her daughter, with only a trace of gray wisps. Her skin was just as flawless, if perhaps a little darker. Their eyes were different. Where Liara had a bright twinkle, her mother held a calculating stare. She looked like she could be cruel if she so wished to be.

Her dress looked regal. Atop her head was a crown made of laurels; bright, pink flowers that almost seemed to glow. Along her wrists were bracelets of various colors and materials, from stark white opals to fiery agates, from rosewood to iron. She wore a long, voluminous robe that did little to hide she was a gorgeous woman with a solid frame that made her look no older than a twenty-year-old.

"You may leave us, Liara," said the mother in a cool tone. "I wish to talk with our guest before I make her large again."

"Yes, mother," said Liara. And then, as she was leaving, looked to Katherine and said, "You'll be fine."

The door shut, leaving the shrunken woman with the giantess.

"You may call me Daphne," said the woman as she slowly walked over. The dresser was tall, so her face was level with Katherine's shrunken, horribly vulnerable body. "My daughter seems to have taken quite an interest in you."

"She's a very sweet girl," said Katherine, unsure what else to say.

"That she is. Come." Daphne picked her up and brought her over to the bed, which was twice the size as Liara's. She deposited her in the center and then stepped back. "I knew a human once. A long time ago. A female, much like you."

"Oh?"

"She would visit from time to time but one day she simply stopped coming. I grew very sad. For the longest time, I shunned your world."

"I'm sorry that happened. Perhaps she moved away?"

"More than likely died," said the woman harshly. "That was many years ago, and we do not age as you do."

"I'm . . . I'm sorry," said Katherine.

"No matter." She moved to the door and Katherine saw her reach out and turn the lock before facing the bed again. "I will grow you back, but I'd like you to . . . indulge me first."

"Indulge you how?"

Daphne didn't say anything, only lifted her laurel crown off and placed it on the dresser. She wiggled her shoulders until the robe fell to the floor, leaving in its place the most luscious skin Katherine had ever seen. Daphne's breasts were exquisite, her pussy shaved, stomach toned. The only thing she was lacking was a navel, but it was hardly noticed. She began to slowly walk toward the bed, her hands outstretched, palms filling with light. Daphne was mouthing a spell.

She brought one leg up to the bed, and then another, walking across it by her knees. Katherine was lying toward the rear, watching this giant woman come closer. But then, her mouth stopped, she threw her head back in soft joy, then a hand was between her legs, gently massaging her pussy. As she drew nearer, Katherine could tell that she'd shrunk a little. With each step closer the goddess grew smaller until she was able to stand and walk to Katherine.

Without a word, Daphne buried her face between Katherine's legs, still shrinking. Katherine could feel her tongue, wet and giant but slowly inching smaller. With each second that passed, Daphne could no longer reach the same spot. It was a pleasure the human girl had never known. When the tongue inevitably got too small, Daphne took to licking along her slit, the face disappearing beneath her. That was when Katherine realized she wasn't shrinking to be equal sized, but shrinking to become even smaller. This was going to be interesting.

Daphne's hands disappeared around Katherine's thighs, drawing up, becoming tiny. Soon the whole woman was vanishing, the bracelets clinking into piles next to Katherine's legs. With the woman becoming less and less, so too did her tongue and lips. For a moment Katherine couldn't feel anything, but then those tiny hands were pushing apart her pussy lips. The human made a coo as she felt the shrunken woman enter her.

She reached back and grabbed the headboards because this was the most intense thing she'd ever felt. A warmth spread throughout her body as the fairy dildo found places that no man (or woman) had ever found in her life. It was pure. It was raw. It was driving her mad because there inside her was a tiny woman, flailing arms, doing summersaults and twirls to get her off. And it didn't take long. Katherine felt her stomach muscles contract as she lifted off the bed, screamed, and then expelled the shrunken woman in a squirt of her juices.

Katherine was worried she'd hurt the shrunken fairy but when she looked down, the tiny woman was starting to grow back, licking the cum off her fingers. The other hand was between her legs, working her own clit. Katherine moved back against the headboard to give the woman room to grow. When she was equal-sized, she leaned over, grabbed Katherine around the neck and pulled her in for a deep kiss. She could taste herself on the fairy and once more brought a tingle to her insides.

Daphne stood up and pulled Katherine to her feet. When they were side by side, she could see that the fairy was about a foot taller. She looked at Katherine, wiping the juices out of her eyes. "I want you to do something for me. Imagine yourself as tall as I am. Feel it in your gut and wish it. Do it now."

Katherine did as the fairy asked, thinking of how nice it would be to grow a little taller, to be equal to the mother of Liara. It was a silly notion because she had no power, but the moment she envisioned it, her feet stretched across the wood, her legs lengthened and her torso expanded. In one quick hiccup, she was standing eye to eye with the fairy.

"What? How? How did that happen?" she asked. Daphne had moved over to a wash basin and was cleaning the cum out of her hair and off her face.

"I put a little magic in you when I was inside you. If you want to grow back to normal, you can on your own."

"So I have . . . the power of size now?"

"As long as you're near the tree, yes." The gears were turning in Katherine's head and Daphne quickly said, "No, not here! If you're going to grow, go outside."

Katherine glanced at the door and subconsciously covered herself. Daphne opened the dresser and found her a bright blue shirt and matching leggings. After, she opened the door and Katherine followed her down the steps to a large common room where Liara waited amongst five other girls. They all looked up at Daphne with reverence and respect.

"I want you to look after our guest. She may decide to stay for a visit." And with that, Daphne said no more and left. Liara came up and hugged Katherine and then introduced her to the five girls—Clara, Adonna, Shana, Trina, and Neema.

"So she . . . gave you fairy magic?" asked Liara as the girls crowded around.

"That's what she said. I was able to grow a little bit just by thinking about it."

Liara looked at the others and then back to Katherine. "Do you think you can shrink too? Fairy magic and humans is a weird thing."

"I don't know," Katherine said. "I'll try."

Once again she envisioned a size—very small, and felt it in the pit of her stomach. At first she didn't think she would be able to do it, that Daphne had only made a way for her to return to normal size. But only a moment of seeing the image being tiny in her head and Katherine felt her feet leave the ground beneath the seat, felt the blue clothing falling off her dwindling frame. The world disappeared in a mass of silk.

Next, a giant hand fished her out of the shirt and placed her on top of it. Six enormous faces crowded around, each more beautiful than the next. Katherine found it slightly intimidating but they were looking at her in a lustful way that made her want to finger herself right there on display. This was an excellent power to have.

Liara looked at the other girls and then back to the shrunken human. "I like this. Will you stay for a little while?"

"I suppose so," said Katherine. She really had no other place to be.

"Good. Because I think we're going to have so much fun!"

Gym Formula

Sandra

She had been going to Hatfield's Gym in Queens
for the last two years and was happy with the results she'd
made. Sandra was already a tall girl—massively tall—
almost six and a half feet, so when she decided to pack on a
little extra muscle, it made her look more like a Greek
goddess than a lumpy giantess. The men loved her. The
women loved her. Whenever she walked by to grab a pair
of dumbbells from the rack, the whole room turned to stare.
She was uncommonly large, but it was starting to be a
problem.

No matter how much muscle she gained from her
rigorous workout, it could not negate the added fat. Sandra
loved to eat—pasta was her weakness. And cookies. And
chocolate. Anything that tasted sweet. Being in the gym
had sent her metabolism through the roof, but it still wasn't
enough. She was sprouting 'love handles' on her waist. Her
jeans weren't fitting anymore. Sandra worried that the
reason women didn't talk to her now wasn't because they
were intimidated but because they weren't attracted.

To make matters worse, Sandra's sister was coming
in at the end of May and the two were going to the beach
for a week. She'd already browsed online for the perfect
swimsuit—a two-piece bikini with bright pink spots on a
black background. Somehow, she thought it would make
her look even taller. But none of that mattered if her fat ass
didn't lose a little bit of weight. She was currently pushing
two-ninety-five, which sounded absolutely massive. Sandra
reminded herself that she was almost seven feet tall. Still,
some of that weight had to come off.

She'd just entered the locker room, ready to head to
the shower when she saw her favorite person sitting on the
bench, lacing up shoes that were comically small. And by

favorite, Sandra meant favorite person to pick on, to ridicule. In no way would little Kristy be her friend.

"What's up, shrimp?" she said, pushing the woman back hard enough to knock her off the bench. "Oops, sorry girl. Let me help you." She picked her up by the shoulders and sat her back on the seat as if she were a child.

"Thanks," said Kristy, although the girl hardly ever made eye contact. They were the same age, but no one would ever suspect it. They both went to the same high school, both graduated the same year, and both stayed only a quarter of a mile from the gym. But they were different in almost every way.

"Nice shoes," said Sandra. "Do they come in adult sizes?"

Kristy finally looked up, fighting back tears. "You know, you don't always have to be such a bitch." She stood up, and for a minute Sandra thought the little tart was actually going to hit her or push her. Instead, she grabbed her towel and headed out to the main floor.

After Sandra showered and dressed, she headed out. She worked as a receptionist at a law office just down the street and it was easy for her to stop at the gym and get ready there after her workout. That was the great thing about Queens—everything you could possibly want was within walking distance.

She'd just pushed the door open, ready to walk out into the busy street and warm air when a bright flyer on the bulletin board in the vestibule caught her eye. Sandra let the door shut and she stood there, reading the colorful ad that someone had placed amongst the lost dogs, babysitting services, and meal supplements ads.

It was for a product called GYM DOWN and it boasted a proven, doctor-recommended supplement that built muscle and trimmed fat. It was the weight-loss drug for the aspiring athlete. All you had to do was take one pill a day and by six weeks, according to the testimonies, the weight shed off like water. Sandra grabbed a business card from the flyer's little pocket and stuffed it into her bag. For the price, it should've been legit. Besides, her current supplement was about to run out and that stuff hardly worked anyway. Maybe it was time to try this new stuff?

Kristy

Oh, how she despised that girl.

Kristy had gone to school with Sandra, and although the amazon probably didn't remember it, had been a horrible bully. For all her life, Kristy had been small, meek, and the punching bag for girls like Sandra. When she hit ninth grade, she stopped growing at five-feet tall. Now, almost twenty-five years old, she was still the same size. Her little arms were almost laughable, especially to a powerhouse like Sandra.

The gym floor was full of towering beauties and ripped men who would never look her way twice. She felt so invisible here, and for the most part that's exactly what she was, because there were few things she could do. Kristy often walked at a mild pace on the treadmill, just enough to keep her heartrate up. Sometimes she'd use the elliptical and every now and then, when the gym was empty, she'd try to lift weights. That was a joke in itself.

Kristy could barely lift the ten-pound weights. Even then, she struggled, her arms shaking wildly like two long pieces of spaghetti. They were so scary and she found herself gingerly placing them back on the rack after managing less than a whole set. How did these gym buffs lift them repeatedly? How did they lift the big one—what was it called? The barbell? She found it exhilarating to watch someone hoist it over her head and then slam it down where it bounced loudly. Kristy was almost certain she'd never get one of those off the ground, even if it was just a bar.

But Sandra . . .

That girl could lift the big ones. And although Kristy was unsure of the weight the Amazonian pressed, she was sure it was a couple hundred. Kristy had watched from the corner once, while on a recumbent bike as Sandra lifted a barbell over her head, the weights stacked across like giant cookies. Her arms shuddered for just a moment and then she was done, a wide grin upon her face.

The worst part of it all? Kristy was totally attracted to her. Who in their right mind wouldn't be? Sandra was a goddess—and although she had been packing on extra weight in the spots where no one ever wanted it—she was still one of the most gorgeous creatures Kristy had ever laid eyes upon. And then there were the feet . . . Kristy was the rare female with a foot fetish, and Sandra hit all the right buttons—hers were large and wide, probably size twelves in women's, with long toes. Kristy fantasized about putting her face against those soles every day that she bumped into the mini-giantess, which was about four times a week. Unfortunately the lust was always overshadowed by Sandra's mean-spiritedness.

Kristy did her workout for the next hour, splitting her time between the recumbent bike and a spot doing yoga where she could watch television. She didn't really commit to the whole workout routine like some people did, certainly not to the degree of Sandra. But, since heart-disease ran in her family, Kristy promised her mom that she would try to exercise more often. When her mom paid for a gym membership, she made sure to come almost every day, knowing it was a far more extravagant gift than her mother could afford.

She didn't have to work today—her shift at the YMCA was on backup call only—so she took her time getting dressed and walking out. But in the vestibule, a brightly-colored flyer garnered her attention. It read GYM UP and was some sort of supplement. While Kristy didn't care much for crazy fads, this one promised something she'd never seen in a gym enhancement before— guaranteed to add inches. Inches? Like in height? It sounded too good to be true, and that was almost always the case. Still, she found herself taking a business card and stuffing it into her back pocket before she left.

Sandra

She'd been taking the supplement for over a week now and barely noticed a difference. When she stepped on the scale it only told her she'd lost two pounds. That was most likely due to the change in diet. In addition to the pricy pills, she had made the commitment to cut back to twenty-three-hundred calories and do away with almost all refined sugars. It was so hard, especially the headaches in the beginning, but she simply started drinking coffee, something she hated with a passion, but now felt necessary to offset her need for caffeine.

More than once she thought about flushing the blue pills down the toilet. Most likely they were placebos. She believed this mainly because of their sweet taste, like little pieces of candy and not a revolutionary enhancement drug. But then she considered the cost and didn't see the hurt in continuing. She would finish the bottle and make her next online purchases with a little more wisdom and foresight.

She had just stepped off the weight bench when she saw little Kristy standing over top of her, looking down at her shoes.

"What? You wanna kiss them?" asked Sandra, crinkling her toes but knowing Kristy couldn't see them. The girl seemed to blush at this, then started to walk off but Sandra was quick to snatch her by the arm. "Why are you so weird? Why are you always staring at me?"

"I'm sorry," she said in a sheepish voice. "I don't mean to be. You're just . . ."

"Just what?" asked Sandra. "Just what?"

Kristy shrugged, looking like she wished more than anything to disappear in that instant. "Pretty?"

Sandra released her arm. "Eww. Gross. I don't swing that way," she said. "Get lost."

Kristy didn't say another word, just dropped her head, gathered her things, and then scampered off to the elliptical.

In truth, Sandra very much swung that way, but she was still coming to terms with it. She'd seen a few women at the gym she would like to experiment with but she was yet to have sex with a female. She'd kissed a few right out of high school but it never went anywhere. She supposed she still liked guys, but there was something about a woman's touch—her smell. She had a foot fetish, but wouldn't dare tell anyone that.

Maybe this was why she didn't care much for Kristy. It was like that little twit could see into her, could recognize that Sandra was a freak. A tall, gargantuan freak who wanted a woman for nothing more than to jam her feet into Sandra's face. The thought of it made her wet so she turned back to the machine she was working and gave it hell.

Later that night, she was reading the warning label on her bottle of GYM DOWN. It gave the usual list of medical advice, the stuff to keep the parent company out of court should someone overdose or simply not use it correctly. In bright red letters above the dosage it read: NEVER TAKE MORE THAN THE RECOMMENDED DOSAGE. But then again, of course it would say that. These companies had to cover their butts, as her sister would say. They didn't want to get sued. So far, the pills weren't doing much. The beach would soon be upon her whether she wanted it or not. And so would the pink and black bikini. She had a sixty-day supply of the pills. What could it hurt to double-up on the dosage, at least for a little while?

Kristy

A day before Sandra had made the commitment to double up on her pills, Kristy had come to the same conclusion. She wasn't gaining any inches, didn't think the drug did anything at all. So to use them up faster, she decided to take two at a time. Even with the giant, scary label on the back of the bottle, she didn't care. If she were ever going to get a girlfriend, if she were ever going to get the attention of anyone like Sandra, she was going to have to be a little taller. Genetics sucked, she thought. This magical little pill was going to have to do the work for her or else she'd die a five-foot tall elderly woman.

Three days after she'd started to double her dose, she marked her height on the doorframe to her bathroom,

just like her parents had when she was little. After drawing
a line across her head, she pulled out a tape measure and
was astounded to see it read sixty-two inches.

"Five-foot-*two*?" she said aloud. She marked her
height again, made sure her bare feet were flat on the tile. It
was correct. She'd grown two inches in only three days.

The next day at the gym she ran into Sandra, who
only gave a derisive snort in her general direction and said
no more. Kristy felt closer to being eye-to-eye, although
that was a bit of an exaggeration. She'd made herself grow
a mere two inches. It would take about twenty more for that
to be possible. But what if she continued to take a double
dosage?

For the first time she tried the fifteen-pound
weights, and although they were incredibly heavy and she
could barely get them up for a single curl, she thought for
sure her body felt different, stouter. This could be the start
of something grand. Would the pills continue to work if she
took more? What if she tripled the dosage? A part of her
just knew that had to be dangerous, but another part, the
part that wanted to be taller and stronger, really didn't care.

She decided when she went home that night, she
would take three pills. If it made her dizzy or nauseated,
then she would back off entirely. At this point, the reward
was worth the risk. After her usual routine, she dressed and
left the gym. But not before seeing Sandra walk out of the
shower, positively glowing. Kristy didn't think she'd ever
seen the woman look so happy and a part of her admired
the smile. Another part was a little terrified.

Sandra

When Kristy passed by, Sandra gave a derisive snort before heading to the locker room to weigh herself and shower. It was a good thing they'd become in sync with one another—Sandra was often finishing up her sets just as Kristy was coming through the door to hop on whatever kiddie machine she could handle. The girl had zero muscle tone, almost as little fat. She was barely more than a rail. But for some reason, Sandra stared at her anyway. She didn't think Kristy ever showered at the gym, but she did change her shoes before and after the workout, and Sandra couldn't help but stare at her toes through the thin mesh of sock.

Sandra always showered before she weighed herself. It was her belief that once she washed off all the sweat and grime, she would weigh less. Nevermind that her hair probably soaked up an extra pound of water but she still did her best to wring it dry. When she stepped up on the scale, her mouth fell open.

She weighed two-hundred and eighty-four pounds. She'd lost eleven since taking the supplement and she was quite sure the majority of that was after she'd decided to double up on the dosage. When she looked down and placed her hands on her stomach, she didn't feel like she'd lost inches there. No matter. If the weight kept falling off, her pudgy belly would eventually suck back in.

The face in the mirror hadn't changed much either. Sandra was a beautiful girl but she had started to fill out in the last few years. Her sharp chin was rounder now and her one dimple on the left side was almost gone. If the GYM DOWN pills had done anything to the fat in her face, she couldn't tell it. Still, the scale didn't lie. That was enough to motivate her to keep taking the pills. And in fact . . .

Tonight, she would triple the dosage.

Kristy

When she measured her height the next time, she was truly afraid. For a moment, she even considered getting rid of the pills because surely this wasn't good for her body. Was she stretching? Elongating on a molecular level? It didn't make sense—it was almost like those pills were magic, the kind that Jack brought home.

Funny enough, those beans grew a beanstalk. The pills were growing a girl . . .

The morning after she took a triple dose she measured herself, only to find the line had crept four inches taller. Kristy, who'd been an even five-foot-tall her whole life was now five and a half feet. She was taller than her mother now. She stared at herself in the mirror, trying to understand where the inches had come from—she didn't necessarily look taller. It's not as though she grew from the legs or the torso. No, she had expanded in all directions.

Just like when she arrived in Wonderland and tasted that magical potion on the table, Alice said, *I'm opening up like a telescope.*

However, this wasn't a curious feeling. Kristy rather liked it. She balled up her fists and didn't feel as tiny or helpless as she had just a day ago. Sure, she'd only gained half a foot, but what if she continued to take the pills? What if, dare she even think it, take a bigger dosage? So far there had been no adverse side-effects other than the wonderful growing. No sickness, no light-headedness. She didn't see the harm in taking a few more . . .

The only problem she had now was that her clothes weren't fitting correctly. She'd planned to wear her favorite button-up shirt but now her breasts were pushing painfully against the little white buttons. Her most comfy jeans were no better, they could hardly be zipped and she had trouble fastening them. Kristy had to wear sandals because her chucks were painful against her toes. If she had to guess, she thought she'd gone up a whole shoe size.

She bought new shoes before going to the gym that morning because she was determined to do something she didn't think possible. Kristy got there early, before the coffee runners and most employees, selected a barbell, and fitted it with a hundred and fifty pounds. Her tiny body still could barely lift it, but she managed to get it up, do one curl, then slowly, gently, place it back on the mat. She felt accomplished, but it was completely undermined by the laughter she heard behind her.

At first Kristy didn't recognize Sandra. Maybe it was the way she was wearing her clothes—Kristy had never seen her in baggy pants and a loose shirt—or maybe it was because she looked a little shorter. Kristy was certain that her own six-inch size increase was making her overcompensate for the woman's smaller stature, but that wasn't completely the case. No, Sandra was definitely shorter. The size-difference in the two girls should not have been so pronounced, but it certainly was. Had she been dipping into her own pills? And why would she ever want to be shorter?

"Let me show you how it's done," said Sandra, moving across the pad to her own barbell which looked double stacked compared to the laughable one Kristy had tried to curl. Sandra positioned her feet, grabbed the bar, then lifted. At first, Kristy thought she would be successful—she'd lifted this thing countless times before. But not this time. This time the weight seemed to catch Sandra off-balance and she pitched forward, her shins catching on the bar, causing her to fall face-first onto the mat. Had it not been padded, she probably would have broken her nose.

"Bravo," Kristy said, gathering courage from the depths of her soul. She even offered a sarcastic slow-clap. She didn't know if it was her added inches, Sandra's *missing* inches, or a combination of the two.

Sandra stood up, tears in her eyes, blood trickling down her nose from where she'd landed. For a moment Kristy felt her blood turn icy, sure that Sandra was about to rush her, but that didn't happen. She only gave the woman a vehement look and stormed off.

And that's when Kristy realized the taller woman had no clue that she had shrunk, or was continuing to shrink.

Sandra

She crashed through the door of the locker room and slammed right into the chest of a woman on her way out. For once in her life, Sandra looked up at someone, not even realizing that she was much shorter than she had been yesterday. Her eyes were filled with tears and she didn't like this feeling one bit. When she stood in front of the mirror, she felt like screaming because she had the same pudgy face as before.

The scale delighted her, though. She was now down to two-fifty-nine. What kind of pill could make a person lose that much weight in just a few days? She was a little worried it was turning out to be the crystal meth diet. Still, it was having some adverse side-effects. Sandra was too upset at having lost control on the gym floor that she still hadn't picked up on the fact that she was shrinking, and had lost almost five inches since the night before. The only thing Sandra saw, and cared about, was that she was feeling weak, and still not losing the fat from her stomach and face.

Before she left, she made sure Kristy was gone for the day. There were two halves of the women's locker room and they often kept to opposite corners so they didn't have to see each other. Sandra dressed, not caring or noticing that her clothes were falling off, that her toes didn't even come close to the ends of the sneakers, and then left.

That night she sat alone in her living room, watching television (some show about a guy handing out roses to a dozen women) and eating ice cream right out of the tub. She was crying but it was certainly unrelated to what happened today. Her nose hurt when she thought about how embarrassed she'd been.

After she finished her snack, she sat there in her bra and panties, happy that they felt loose, but sad that her body still looked the same. The sight of her fat rolls bunching up along her stomach as she sat made her cringe, and she moved to another chair so that she could sit straighter. Still, the puffiness of her body was upsetting and she couldn't help but look over and then, after a brief consideration, take the bottle of pills. She still didn't make the connection, only believed that she was getting thinner. She just needed to train harder.

She swallowed five pills.

Kristy

Likewise, Kristy swallowed five pills.

The next day at the gym was rather unique. Perhaps the higher dosage lengthened the effects because at the beginning of the day, she'd only grown an additional two inches. She was creeping close to the six-foot mark, something that was a huge milestone for her because that seemed to be the height of many of her guy friends. It was an exhilarating thought to be able to look them directly in the eye when talking. By her estimates, she should've shot up at least three more inches.

In the gym that day Kristy managed to lift a barbell with almost two-hundred pounds of weights. She lifted it twice, then dropped it. She felt her strength was increasing exponentially because it wasn't that she was just getting taller—she was getting bigger. Her arms, her legs, her muscles and bones. It was all making her powerful. She hiccupped, and felt her body change, but only a little. While watching the ground, she saw her feet creep longer. By now, she wasn't wearing shoes because she didn't know what size she'd need. Today's shoes wouldn't fit tomorrow's feet.

"What the hell?" asked a voice behind her.

Kristy turned around and saw her rival, but it didn't click that she was standing on the same platform—she thought the once Amazonian had to be a step down because they were nearly eye-to-eye. Sandra looked awful. She was sweating profusely, her clothes hanging off her. She kept one hand cinched around the waistband of her pants, as if they'd fall down should she let go.

"Jesus, what's wrong with you?" asked Kristy.

"I don't . . . I don't . . . you're taller!" she managed to get out.

"Uh huh," said Kristy, not pointing out the fact that they were splitting the difference. The oblivious woman hiccupped, and right before her eyes, Sandra began to shrink. It was slow at first, but the constant stare the two had been sharing broke, and it was unmistakable that Sandra's eyes were sliding out of view, and the woman was having to look up.

She turned around, ran off to the locker room with her feet stumbling over each other. It was the most amazing thing to see because the woman, who once towered over her, was quickly becoming smaller than Kristy had originally stood. Kristy looked around, made sure no one was watching, then followed Sandra into the locker room.

It was empty, and that was a blessing because things were about to get weird.

Sandra

She realized it wasn't weight that she was losing. She was losing inches, mass, size. All of the above. As freakish as it sounded, Sandra was shrinking. When she rounded the corner, she fell over the doorway into the locker room. There were no others there, and for that she was glad because she was first embarrassed, and second scared to be seen. As she got to her feet, it was as if the whole room had changed. The ceiling was further up, the bank of showers further back. She was dragging her shoes because her feet no longer fit in them. By the way her clothes were bunching up around her ankles, the shoes were stuck and she couldn't kick them off.

By the time she made it over to the bench, she was no more than half her size. It was at this point she regretted taking so many of the pills. The drug never was a weight-loss, muscle-building supplement. It was to take away inches, plain and simple. And like a moron, Sandra had taken way more than she needed to take. Her breathing was labored and she worried her lungs may collapse because it felt like the world was crushing her. Her little hands gripped the bench and she watched her fingers slide across, disappearing into the fabric of her shirt, and then she was shrinking down, down, down . . .

Now, she was surrounded by her own scent. It was strong, sweaty, and wet. Clearly she'd shrunken down so small that she disappeared into her own shoe. Thank God that it ended here, she thought. For a moment she worried that she may shrink away to nothing.

The ground shook but she couldn't see anything. It was dark inside the sneaker with all the clothes that fell on top of her after she'd shrunk. She held her chest as she wrestled her way out of a sock. Still, the shoe and the sweaty shirt were keeping her from escaping. Sandra could see movement above her, could see a dark shape blot out the impossibly high overhead lights and then, her sweaty prison grew bright.

A giant face looked down at her, sweat dripping and landing in the shoe. Kristy stared at the shrunken girl with a mixture of wonder and glee. Sandra couldn't fathom such size—it wasn't just that she'd shrunken down. Now, she realized that Kristy had added a few inches. At this size, that hardly mattered, but it was clear now that they'd both ingested drugs they probably shouldn't have.

"What happened, girl?" asked Kristy, moving the clothes aside so she could get a better look at the cowering, naked woman. Then she was rifling around in Sandra's gym bag next to the pile of clothes until she pulled out the large bottle of GYM DOWN. "So your pills are blue? What did you think this stuff was? Weight loss?"

Sandra said nothing, just looked down and tried to cover her nakedness.

"Why on earth would you want to lose weight?" asked Kristy. It was a nicer, more humble question than

Sandra would have guessed her capable of. "You had an amazing body. Most of us would kill for it."

"Get me help, please!" said the shrunken girl. "I don't want to be stuck this way."

"Not sure if you get the option, doll," said Kristy. "Maybe if you ah, oh . . ."

Her voice trailed off and she laid her head back against the locker. Sandra tried to see from the floor what was happening but it was difficult. The bench was making a groaning sound as Kristy's head moved up. She was growing—right there in the locker room, she was growing larger. Sandra felt her own prison shift and then quickly she was moving across the floor as Kristy's giant, sweaty foot came hurtling toward her. Whatever drug Kristy had taken, Sandra wished she had a little bit for herself. Could it reverse what had happened?

"Oh, that one felt nice," said Kristy, running fingers through her hair. "I think I'm about as tall as you now. Well, as tall as you *were*."

"Please. You have to help me," said Sandra, feeling her heart sink by how casual the whole experience was to Kristy.

"Maybe. You've been pretty shitty to me, do you realize that?" she asked the shrunken woman. Kristy brought her face close and it frightened Sandra by how much she'd changed in just a few minutes.

"I'm sorry. Just please. Call someone. My sister's number is in my cellphone in my bag."

"Maybe later," said Kristy. "C'mon. Let's get out of here."

"What? What do you mean?" She didn't finish her thought because Kristy pulled out one of Sandra's sweaty gym socks, held it open, then dropped the shrunken woman inside it. She flailed around, fought with the fibers to get out but the giantess had cinched the top. Sandra felt the cool air filtering through as she was deposited somewhere. By the smell of things, it was probably her own gym bag

And then, she was moving.

Kristy

The first thing she did when she got home was measure herself against the doorframe. This had been a big growth spurt, one that made her abnormally large, but she didn't care. She'd put on Sandra's sneakers and even those were too small. Her toes scrunched up at the end and it made walking painful. Hopefully no one thought it odd— this nearly seven-foot woman walking home with two gym bags, one containing a tiny, four-inch woman.

And seven-foot was almost where her size had landed. She only lacked three inches until that mark. Kristy now stood about three inches taller than where Sandra had stood only a week ago. It was almost cumbersome to move around her apartment—her head nearly brushed the doorways and she was going to have to sit on the toilet sideways because her knees were too close to the bathtub.

She turned her attention back to the shrunken woman in the gym bag. After finding the writhing, bickering sock, Kristy turned it upside down and deposited the little woman on her coffee table.

"What the hell!" she screamed, looking around. "You brought me to your house?" She looked adorable, this once Amazonian warrior now reduced to nothing more than a toy.

"Sure did," said Kristy. "I think it's about time I get reparations for how you've treated me over the past year."

"You can go to hell," said the little woman.

Kristy's hand lashed out and shoved the woman over with little effort. She was angry, got back up and rushed to the edge of the table where Kristy shoved her over once again. The giant woman giggled and sat back, folding her arms across her chest. "You gonna keep giving me attitude? Or do I need to flick you across the room?"

"What do you want?" Sandra said, a little calmer, crossing her own arms across her chest in a standoffish way.

"Well first I'd like to hear an apology."

"I'm sorry," she said without hesitating.

Kristy rolled her eyes and shook her head. "I don't believe that one. Try again."

Sandra stared up at her with hate-filled eyes, then mouthed her response with a low, guttural growl. "I'm sorry I was mean to you. Please forgive me."

"I'm sure I will in time. For now, I have a use for you."

"A use?"

Kristy put her feet up on the coffee table, and at this size they were easily three-times as long as the shrunken woman. "I want you to rub them."

Sandra

"No way," she answered, even though it was a turn on to be so close to them, to feel their heat and smell their scent. She was beyond feeling aroused. Now, she was just angry that this little twat was treating her like nothing more than a pet.

"No way?" the giantess repeated? "Okay, then."

She dropped her feet to the floor and started pulling down her tight sweatpants. Peeling off was more like it, as Kristy's growth spurt back at the gym had left her nearly bursting through her clothes. The giantess picked up the shrunken woman and then rotated on her sofa so that she lay on her back. In the next moment Sandra was standing between her legs, Kristy's giant pussy twice as long as her whole body.

"Get in there," the giantess ordered.

"What? You can't be serious," said Sandra.

"Too long," said Kristy, then scooped up the small woman and shoved her right in. Sandra tried to fight it, but Kristy held herself open with two fingers and pushed the tiny woman against the back. It was wet and warm but smelled and tasted divine. Kristy moved around, and each time she did Sandra felt herself being pulled deeper inside. The light vanished and she was left inside a tight, disorienting cell that muffled all sounds besides an otherworldly heartbeat.

She wanted to be angry—she should've been downright livid—but she couldn't bring herself to feel that way. This was fucking hot. She was enjoying it far too much to stay mad for long. Sandra felt weightless inside Kristy, so she rode the wave of flesh, fingering herself and hoping that when the giantess erupted, the orgasm wouldn't be so massive that it drowned her. Kristy was difficult to get off, so Sandra managed to spend at least twenty minutes inside, tossed around until the walls went rigid, a moan somewhere far off intensified, and a torrent of warm juices flushed her out.

Sandra sat up on the leather sofa and coughed, then ran a hand across her face to clear the giantess's cum. The air was so much cooler outside, and she had just caught her breath when giant finger grabbed her beneath the arms and placed her back on the table. Sandra got to her feet and looked up at the now fully naked Kristy, skin blotched from the orgasm.

"Now," said the giantess. She placed her feet back up on the glass. "You can rub, but since you didn't want to work earlier, you have a new task. Lick them clean."

Sandra didn't argue, knowing that the giant woman could make her do whatever she wished. But also, it was a turn on. Sandra was past the point of caring. She was fearful for her own life, not just what Kristy could do to her but also what the supplement had already done to her body. Could this even be reversed? She couldn't live her whole life being a mere four inches tall.

Kristy's skin tasted so good—the saltiness of her sweat was intoxicating. Sandra must have done a good job because an hour later, with a sore jaw and hands, the giantess plucked her off the table and took her to the bathroom. Kristy stoppered the sink and drew hot water inside, then placed a bar of soap next to the edge.

"Bathe," she told the tiny woman, then hopped in the shower.

Kristy

It was invigorating feeling a tiny woman struggle inside of her. As she turned on the showerhead and pulled the curtain, her fingers found her sweet spot again, bringing her to another orgasm, albeit a little disappointing. She could get used to having a shrunken woman play inside her pussy.

She bathed, washed her hair, and shaved her legs. The shrunken woman did likewise, minus the shaving. Kristy watched her sit in the sink basin of hot water, which came up to her chest. It was as if she were checked out, probably more afraid than she'd ever been in her life. It was a scary concept being so small, but Kristy couldn't relate, nor did she want to try. She liked having this little pet around, and didn't know where she should take the adventure from here.

Clearly the police would have something to say about all this. After all, this was mild kidnapping. Then Sandra could also spin the whole thing as rape, even if she did enjoy it immensely. Kristy had done a bad thing, which meant she had two choices—she could either come clean, end the adventure and possibly face jail time. Or, she could continue to be bad, take care of the shrunken woman and have a human fucktoy whenever she needed it.

Kristy pulled back the shower curtain and looked down at the woman. Sandra looked up, met her gaze, and offered a weak smile.

Kristy thought, *How hard could it be to care for a shrunken woman anyway?*

Olympic Formula

The Follow-Up to Gym Formula

"It's gonna be six-hundred dollars a bottle," said the shady guy behind the van window. She wasn't entirely sure but she thought his name was Fred.

"Six-hundred? That's insane!" said Molly, but she was digging around in her purse just the same.

Fred flicked a cigarette out the window. Their vehicles were close, almost touching, and Molly had even rented a car so that hers wouldn't be recognized. She hated coming to this part of town, but it was now or never. She'd be on a plane later tonight.

"This stuff went off the market as soon as that lady shrunk that girl and held her against her will. It's powerful stuff. You can get arrested just for having it."

"I know, I know," said Molly, handing him a wad of cash, enough for two bottles of each—The GYM UP and GYM DOWN formula. "I read the papers."

And what a story it had been.

A pharmaceutical company had created a new weight loss and weight gain supplement that had very odd side-effects: It could make a person shrink or grow. This side-effect wasn't known until the drug was abused, and since it was marketed to fitness buffs, the abuse came early. Reports of people shrinking or growing several feet dominated the news for a few weeks after the products launched, but none were as popular as the girls Kristy and Sandra who frequented a gym together in New York.

Kristy had been bullied by Sandra—Molly remembered her saying as much during the trial. She'd taken some of the supplement and began to grow, topping out at over seven feet. Meanwhile, Sandra, who wanted to lose a little puffiness in her face and waist, started taking the supplement that made her shrink. Both girls abused the product, and after it was over, Sandra was Kristy's captive, and the poor girl was only a few inches tall. Something about that story gave Molly an idea, and hope. She was pretty certain it was the case for everyone else who'd thought about growing and shrinking.

That night she caught a plane headed to London where she would be competing in the Mini Olympics—a once a year event that showcased the best runners and swimmers in the world. What that translated to, in Molly's opinion, was that it showcased the best runners and swimmers who couldn't make it to the *actual* Olympics. That was fine with Molly. It was still a prestigious award to be won, and it put her in line to one day compete in the real games. But she had two little problems.

The first one was easy to solve now that she had bottles of the GYM UP formula. Molly was still a little too short. She was barely above five feet, and in the business of swimming, every inch counted. She'd been scouring the dark web for anyone who had experience overdosing on the formula and found a few similarities. For every three pills she took, she gained two inches. Tonight, when she arrived at her hotel, she'd take fifteen and hope they didn't kill her. Besides, all of her other clothes were brand new and scaled to her hopeful size. She was banking on this being successful.

Her second problem, or problems rather, were two girls: Lola and Penny. Both were swimmers, both on her team, and both in the bottom for every event. If she could somehow knock them out, it would move her up considerably during the qualifying swim. She had a plan, she just hoped it would work. A large part of it relied on luck.

After the plane touched down that evening, she had a light dinner, called her sister back in Wyoming, then settled in for the night. She had a pair of sleep shorts that were incredibly loose, but hopefully not for much longer. On her room service tray was the bottle—the same bottle that would have her arrested for so much as possessing—and fifteen pills counted out into a pile.

One after another, she popped them into her mouth, followed by a swig of water. They had an earthy sort of aftertaste, and as she swallowed the fifteenth and final tablet, she felt like she'd be sick. Molly padded her way to the bathroom sink, turned on the light and looked at her reflection in the mirror, waiting and hoping for a change. Those websites she'd found online all said it took just a few minutes, and almost none of them claimed you would die soon after. But then again, if she wanted a big reward, she had to take a big risk.

Horrible waves of pain hit her stomach and she thought she was going to vomit. She concentrated on winning the event and pushed the sick feeling out of her mind. But soon after the stomach cramps went away, she looked down at her feet and watched, amazed, as her toes stretched across the cold tile floor. Her fingers, which were digging painfully into the sink basin, started to elongate, making little popping sounds as they grew longer. Molly watched her reflection in the mirror, watched as it rose higher, watched as her breasts pushed out further. After a few minutes of slow, steady growth, the feeling was almost pleasurable.

She wished she'd brought a tape measure to see how accurately she'd predicted her growth but settled with trying on her new swimsuit. It was fitting perfectly—so she'd guessed correctly. Right now, Molly stood at nearly six feet tall. The pills had given her an additional ten inches, and if she need to, she'd take even more.

The next morning, she met her teammates in the private pool owned by the hotel. It was an Olympic-sized pool, regulation standard, and that was the whole reason their manager had decided to put them there. Molly had overslept, and when she opened the door, the hot air of the pool blasting her in the face, she was met with wide-eyes and open jaws.

"Were you always so tall" asked Penny, the lanky, gorgeous blond who had a needlessly ridiculing tone.

"Yeah, for real!" said Lola, just before she jumped in the pool and butterflied away.

Molly just shrugged, dropped her gym bag, then hopped in the water. She had a new body, one that actually weighed about thirty pounds more than it did yesterday, and she had to learn how to move in the water all over again. Luckily it didn't take long—if anything she moved faster now, and perhaps wouldn't even need to launch part two of her plan.

But where was the fun in that?

The girls decided to do a warmup race and naturally Molly finished third. She wasn't anywhere near as swift as these girls, had not been swimming nearly as long, and certainly didn't have the drive that either true athletes held. But Molly had ingenuity, and sometimes that's what mattered most.

"Why are you even here?" asked Penny later as they were drying off. She bumped Molly so hard that the girl almost fell into the water.

"You aren't even going to place," added Lola. "You're like six seconds down from us, and I'm the slowest on the team!"

"I'll get in there, just you wait," said Molly, knowing that she would certainly qualify two days from now. She watched the girls walk off, smiling. They were headed to the gym, just as they did after any swim. They were so predictable, and that was going to cost them in the end.

***

That night, Molly took a cab to a town about thirty minutes outside of London. She didn't want to be spotted making her odd purchases because to the observing eye, it would leave a trail back to Molly. Her first stop was to a convenience store where she bought two bottles of water— the overpriced drinks that were global enough for her to find in another country. One was called Beach, and the other was called Maui. After that, she visited a tiny pet store and picked up a small, metal bird cage.

Later, alone in her room, she started the arduous process of twisting the GYM DOWN tablets into a small bowl, filling it with a yellowish powder and then throwing the plastic capsule away. After she'd gone through the entire two bottles—some four-hundred capsules, she had a whole bowl full of what looked like cornmeal. She didn't know how much she needed for the desired results, she actually didn't know what the desired results would be. So she dumped a large swig from each of the bottles and then split the difference. Each of tall drinks now had a whole bottle's worth of shrinking stuff in it. When it dissolved, the water was still crystal-clear. She sniffed, and couldn't detect any odor at all. Hopefully there wouldn't be a taste either.

She packed them into her gym bag and placed it by the door. As she went to bed, listening to the odd sounds of a strange, foreign city, she was smiling. This was definitely going to work.

The next day, she went for a swim alongside the girls, listening to them chastise her speed, her form, her looks. They could be cruel women and at times Molly didn't even know why she was trying so hard. Part of it was the attraction—she loved women, and of course Lola and Penny were two of the most attractive. She didn't think they swung that way, perhaps Lola, but certainly not Penny. Molly had been out with the girls before and saw the disgust her eyes when another woman tried to buy her a drink.

After the swim, they trotted off to the gym, but this time Molly decided to go with them.

"Can you even lift weights with your little bony arms?" asked Lola on the way over.

"Geez, I just want to ride the bike. Why is everything such a hassle with you two?"

"Because for some reason you think you can just barge into the winner's circle," said Penny. "That's not happening. You shouldn't even be on this trip."

"Well I'm sorry you feel that way," she said, entering the gym.

There was no one else inside, and that was a very good thing. The girls sat their gym bags down and while Lola and Penny went to change in the locker room, Molly stayed beyond, pretending to stretch. She was delighted to see both girls first pull out their water bottles, take a swig, then return them to their bags. Molly was also glad that the bottle styles were the same, so this little plan was going to come off without a hitch.

As soon as the girls disappeared around the corner, Molly grabbed the spiked water from her bag, then quickly replaced them with what was in the girls' bags. Then she put their water with her belongings and threw her towel across to hide them. Easy as could be. Now, she had to figure out how to manage the girls when the change finally did happen. If the stories online were true, she might get lucky.

They returned, now dressed in workout gear and running shoes. Lola grabbed her water and headed to the weight bench. Penny grabbed hers and found the rowing machine. Both had chosen spots so they could watch the wall-mounted televisions which were currently covering the Mini Olympics. Molly chose the recumbent bike so she could watch the girls as they slowly, but steadily drank their water. At every workout, the girls always threw their bottles in the trash on the way out, accustomed to drinking a whole one during their hour-long routine.

As Lola's bench pressing went on, Molly could tell the woman was slowly getting smaller. She kept pulling up her wristbands, kept pulling her foot out of her shoe and tying the laces tighter. When she stumbled, expecting the weight of her barbell to be much lighter than it was, Penny stopped rowing and looked over at her friend with quizzical, yet concerned eyes.

"Are you okay?" she asked, pulling her earbud out.

"I'm fine," said Lola, stretching and then settling for the dumbbells on the rack. She selected two, and by the way her arms dropped, it was clear she wasn't expecting them to be so heavy. Embarrassed, she looked around, expecting both sets of eyes to be upon her but Penny had gone back to rowing and staring at the television while Molly was careful to be looking at her phone.

Meanwhile Penny had taken out her earbuds and draped the cord over her shoulders. Although she didn't say it or show it, Molly guessed they'd grown to be painfully large in her ears. Each time she rowed, it was like her clothes moved slower because she wasn't filling them out the same way and the inertia was constantly changing.

Molly kept looking at the door, worried that someone would walk in. She didn't have a game plan if that happened, other than deny any sort of involvement. Still, it would probably be very bad for her if anyone found out. The girls were looking noticeably smaller now, yet neither would stop long enough to assess the situation. They were both so focused on the workout that they didn't seem to see each other. Had Lola looked up, she would've seen Penny swimming in her clothes, fighting to keep the shoes on her feet. And had Penny looked up, she would have seen Lola standing there, in shock, as to why the ten-pound weights were giving her so much trouble when she could easily lift the twenty-five-pound ones yesterday.

Then, just as Molly had hoped, things sped up.

"Oh, *fuck*!" said Lola, the weights dropping to the ground. She was doubled over, holding her stomach. It made it more difficult to notice that she was almost half her size, but when she stood, looked the room over, she found Penny's eyes and the two women knew, all at once.

"You did this, didn't you?" said Penny, standing up. Her clothes were falling off her shoulders and just as she took a threatening step forward, she tripped over the metal frame of the rowing machine and plummeted straight to the ground. Molly gave a tiny giggle, then hopped off the bike.

Penny struggled to get up because she was dwindling away so fast. Lola was gone, now disappeared beneath the mound of her clothes. Molly had to work fast, stepping over the shrinking woman by the rower and heading straight for the girl surrounded by free weights the same size as her. Without even looking, Molly scooped up the pile of clothes and shoes and dumped them into her gym bag.

"You're not going to get away with this, you fucking psycho!" said Penny who was quickly disappearing into the neck hole of her shirt.

Molly grabbed the naked woman as she still dwindled and held her up eye level. The fear in that tiny woman was enjoyable and she knew this was going to be a great bonus to moving up the ranks on the team.

"Careful, you little twat," said Molly. "I was just going to keep you in a cage. But I'll crush the life out of you if I have to."

That made the shrunken woman quite compliant. Although Molly didn't think such torture would be needed, saying it out loud definitely made it an alternative.

***

Molly had been smart enough to take the SIM cards out of the girls' phones and crush them before throwing the devices into the trash. That was the only thing that could link her back to them. Sure, the place had cameras, but would anyone really know she'd shrunken them and kidnapped them? It was plausible, but she felt the odds were in her favor. Both girls had families, but by the time their disappearances were noted, the trail of evidence would be cold.

Later that night in the hotel room, she was about to hop in the shower, but decided against it in favor of a better idea. She had taken the shrunken women, both around six inches tall, and placed them in the wire bird cage. They went through the routine she expected—first they were angry, shouting obscenities and making threats. Then they started to plead, to make deals, to promise to drop out of the Olympics if only she'd make them big again. And finally, they were scared, huddled in the corner and crying against one another.

Molly loved their clothes—she felt like a freak for putting their socks and panties so close to her face, but the scent was driving her crazy. Besides, she'd have to get rid of that stuff anyway, so why not enjoy it while it was here? She stripped down completely, then brought the cage over to sit next to her. The girls looked up at her with frightful eyes, unknowing what was in store. Molly slid up the door and held it there.

"Out," she said.

Both of the tiny naked girls just looked up at her, as if not comprehending. In truth, they were both scared to death. Molly grabbed the cage, turned it on its side, then shook the shrunken women out onto the bed. Their little screams were pitiful, yet enjoyable just the same. It was nice to finally turn the tables on women who'd been so cruel to her over the last few months. Molly couldn't help but smile and lick her lips at the sight of them trying to stand up on the lumpy bed covers.

"What are you going to do with us?" asked Lola.

"You can't treat us like animals," added Penny.

Molly grinned. "I can treat you any way I wish." She rolled over onto her back and then looked down at her shrunken victims. "I want you to massage my feet."

"What?" both girls said in unison.

"You heard me. They're so sore because my shoes aren't fitting quite right just yet. I need to buy some bigger ones."

"You can't expect us to do that," said Lola in a pleading voice.

"You will do that, and your work isn't going to end there. Get to it or this will be a very rough evening for you both."

The tiny women exchanged glances, then looked up at the giantess. Lola appeared willing, but by the way Penny locked her arms and put out her leg, Molly knew she was going to be trouble.

"Come on," Lola pleaded with her tiny friend. "Let's not make trouble."

"No! She can't do that to us! She can't make us massage her sweaty, smelly feet!"

"Actually I can," said Molly, sitting up and snatching the tiny women. She deposited them toward the end of the bed, one at each foot. "And now, for being stubborn that massaging just became a cleaning. Get to licking."

Again, she expected resistance from at least Penny, so Molly brought her feet down on each of the women, pushing them painfully hard against the mattress. She didn't think she would crush them, but the girls didn't know that. Their tiny screams were muffled against the pads of her feet. Little arms tried to smack at her, to push the feet away, but they couldn't.

Finally, after the girls gave up and were still, she moved her feet away and looked down at them. They were crying. Lola rolled over, put her face in her hands and wept.

Penny just had a resigned look in her eyes. Molly flicked them both, startling them but also making them look up at their giantess warden.

"Shall we try again?" She crinkled her toes and realized just how sweaty she'd become.

Both girls rolled around, sat up, then wordlessly nodded. Molly shoved her feet at them again, but gave the girls enough room to work. She laid her head back on the pillow and felt tiny hands and tiny tongues going to work. It felt great, and she draped a dirty sock across her face, feeling herself grow warm, and feeling herself grow wet. If only she had a controlled environment with someone she trusted—Molly wouldn't mind at all to be a tiny woman licking a giant sole.

Her fingers crept below, found her sweet spot and began to rub. She kept moving her feet away from the shrunken women as her back arched, but she kept returning them just as fast. At some point she heard one of their voices say, "God, she's fingering herself! That bitch is getting off on this!"

It had to be Penny, thought Molly. The anti-gay girl who could never touch a female. Licking a giant woman's foot was probably the most dehumanizing thing she'd ever done. Well, so far . . .

Molly grabbed the shrunken women, little yelps screaming out as she dropped them onto her stomach. They stood up on shaky legs, gazing past the giantess's breasts to her smiling face. Penny looked as though she were about to cry while Lola just stared on with silent resignation, as if she had accepted her fate.

The giantess put her fingers on Lola's shoulders and forced her to sit, then flicked her little legs open. Molly said, "Eat her out." For a minute Penny just had a blank look across her face, as Lola had moments ago. The woman probably didn't understand the request, so foreign it was to have sex with a woman.

"What?" she asked, mind sounding foggy.

"I want you to get down and lick her pussy. It's not hard. You just licked a foot, so you can lick a pussy."

"Fuck you, you giant bitch. I'm not doing that!"

Molly had anticipated this and she decided to try an experiment. She twisted one of the GYM DOWN capsules and pushed one half of it into Penny's face. The little woman struggled but it was comical because she fought with the enthusiasm of a kitten. At least a kitten could claw and bite—this miniscule cunt couldn't even do that. She kicked her legs, swatted at Molly's giant fingers but couldn't move the capsule from her face. Little bits of yellow powder fell over the side but for the most part the woman was swallowing it, probably even breathing it. And wasn't a drug more effective when it was inhaled?

Lola just sat where she'd been placed, like a puppet that couldn't move without its puppeteer. When Molly moved the capsule away, a yellow ring surrounded Penny's nose and mouth. She coughed, almost vomited, but Molly flicked her on the back to make sure she wasn't choking. Then, the tiny thing rolled onto her side, arms held tightly around her stomach.

"Oh, God, Oh, *fuck*," she said, sounding in great pain. Lola continued to cry but she was paralyzed with fear.

Then, the six-inch woman in the fetal position began to draw up even more. Her feet contracted, hair got shorter, plump ass smaller. She was shrinking and screaming and crying and Molly couldn't help but be aroused. It was the hottest thing in the world to take someone's power as she had. With such a large dose at such a smalls size, Molly fully expected the woman to shrivel up and disappear. But that didn't happen. She shrank until she was roughly half her size—three inches. That was even better.

Molly picked her up under her arms, feeling as though she could break her ribcage with barely a thought. Even as such a small size, Penny was shaking. Her little legs were hanging limply but they were spasming as if electrified. The big lady deposited her on the bed again, right between the legs of a woman who was now a mini-giantess to her. Both looked at each other, knowing there would be no negotiating out of this.

"Now, let's try this again," said Molly. "Eat her out, or I'll make you so small that she'll fuck your entire body."

"Just do it," cried Lola. "It's better than getting any smaller."

Penny was finally onboard, crawling up Molly's stomach until she reached the giant pussy. Then, she buried her face in it with far more enthusiasm that Molly would have guessed. The smallest woman worked the giant clit, licking, sucking, kissing. Lola threw her head back, enjoying it but knowing she shouldn't. Molly loved watching this—what could be sexier than one mini-woman servicing another mini-woman on your stomach? Molly's fingers drifted below and started working her clit.

Both women came at the same time, the tiny Lola who bit her lip and subconsciously put a hand to her shrunken friend's head, and Molly, whose orgasm was so powerful that it unseated the tiny couple. They came apart, rolled down opposite sides, then landed on the bed. Molly picked them both up, held them up in her hands so she could stare at them. Both were quivering with fear when she brought her eyes to theirs.

"How about some real fun?" she asked them.

"Please just let us go," said Lola. "You can just open your door and we'll leave. We just want out of here."

"I bet you do. That's crazy talk though. It must be really bad here if you'd rather brave the outside world at six- and three-inches tall."

Penny looked as though she wanted to fight, and luckily for Molly that was never going to happen. Sure, it was rumored that enough GYM UP could make someone regain their size (with a multitude of lifelong health issues thereafter) but Molly had no desire to offer them any such help. In fact, she'd grown bored after swimming yesterday and emptied all of the GYM UP formula into a bowl.

"The Olympics isn't worth all this," said Penny, so small that it was almost like hearing a television with the volume all the way down.

"This isn't about the Olympics anymore," said Molly, as much a surprising admission to herself as to the tiny girls. Sure, she wanted to get to the real Olympics, but shrinking down her rivals was its own reward. She held the tiny women in her hands a moment longer, then spread her legs and shoved them into her pussy.

Penny was easy to push inside, she had no ability to fight, no weight to throw around, so Molly simply lined her up and used a finger to shove her through. Lola tried to fight, her appendages flailing wildly. Molly squeezed her legs, trapping the woman halfway inside her—Lola's upper half was hanging out, and the tiny woman was panting, losing the fight. Right now, her feet were probably kicking Penny into oblivion.

Molly shoved half a capsule of GYM DOWN into her mouth. Lola wasn't expecting it, so her mouth had been open in mid-scream and swallowed a lot more than the already miniscule Penny. Lola's body went limp—from defeat or from so much of the drug—Molly couldn't tell. But as her fingers pushed the woman inside, she was already shrinking, her little body folding up like a telescope.

However, there was a little bit of life left in them.

They were moving around, trying to help each other, trying to escape their wet, warm prison. In the process, they were about to make Molly orgasm harder than she'd ever in her life. She rubbed her clit, but wanted to keep her hand close because if she gushed, she'd most likely expel the shrunken people. Molly was writhing on the bed, the little people working her over far more effectively than they probably meant.

When she finally did cum, it gushed between her fingers. But no little people. They weren't moving anymore, and she probably should've felt sad about that but she didn't. After she caught her breath, she reached inside and found the lifeless little people. One at a time, she pulled them out, neither breathing. Lola was now much smaller, no more than an inch tall—Molly was lucky to even find her. She didn't know if they could be saved or not, but she didn't plan on doing mouth-to-mouth. Instead, she balled them up in large wads of toilet paper and flushed them down the toilet.

***

When it came time to compete, Molly actually placed third from the bottom. She could've probably out-swam Lola and Penny either way. No matter. They were considered no-shows for the qualifier, and therefore barred from competing. The other girls were difficult to judge, but no one seemed to think any differently of Molly. She'd gotten away with it, but it wasn't enough. She still had six slots left to go. Could she make more girls disappear? She had one more bottle of GYM DOWN, after all . . .

Over the next week she started a romance with Kendra—the number six girl on the team. She was easy to lure back to the hotel room, to kiss, to go down on, and then to drug. She'd had so much to drink by the time the shrinking stuff took effect that she didn't even realize her body was dwindling away. Molly just watched, fingering herself, as the woman became no more than four-inches tall. While the girl was unconscious, Molly rubbed her on her clit, but in the end, the tiny woman was flushed down the toilet like the rest.

Another girl, Gail, was the lead swimmer on the team. By now, Molly had moved up to number four, and was well-liked by almost everyone. Gail was a holdout, as the number one was in any sport. She feared competition, feared how Molly had effortlessly scaled the ranks due to technicalities. Girls were going missing and although Molly benefitted, no one directly assumed it was her doing. Not yet.

One night, she caught Gail stumbling back to her hotel room, drunk, talking on her cellphone. Molly had come up with a better idea for shrinking, Gail being the lab rat. She crept up behind the woman, and just as she ended her call, jammed a needle into her back and plunged it. She whipped around in surprise, ready to scream out, but saw it was Molly and her face broke down in anger.

"What was that?" she asked, rubbing her back.

"What was what? Sorry, I bumped you a little too hard. Let me walk you to your room."

Gail nodded, slowly, not seeming to buy that explanation, but allowed Molly to escort her. They never made it.

The drug took effect—Molly had mixed it with water and since it went directly into the bloodstream, it worked much quicker. Gail started to fall out of her shoes until she was stumbling from not only the alcohol but also the shrinking. By the time Molly was scooping up her clothes, the woman had dwindled away to nothing. There was no tiny woman to collect. Molly rubbed the carpet, wondering where she could've gone, but the solution must have been far more powerful than she guessed. Molly just took the clothes back to her room and put them in trash bags like all the rest.

***

A night later there was a knock at the door. Molly dubiously stood up and looked out—her heart sinking to see two uniformed police officers. She told herself to be calm and that this wasn't a big deal. There were missing girls on her team, and as such, there would probably be questions. Putting a steadying hand across her chest, she slowed her breathing, then opened the door.

"Molly Russell?" said the first officer.

"Yes?"

"I'm Michael Duncan and this is Timothy Warden," he said, introducing the other man. She found it odd that British officers introduced themselves by their first names rather than by officer. "We have a few questions about your teammates. We would like you to come with us, please."

Come with them? she thought. That was odd protocol. If they wanted to ask questions, why not just ask them here? If she were requested to come with them, what did that mean? The worst-case scenarios were playing in her mind. They knew something. Someone had seen camera footage, a piece of clothing had been found, a witness had watched her talking with any of the seven girls that she'd shrunken down and made disappear. She wanted to scream out internally, but she wouldn't give them the satisfaction.

"Is something wrong?" she asked them.

"Just some questions about your connection to your teammates," said Michael.

"You've been rather fortuitous, wouldn't you say?" said Timothy. "They go missing and you climb the ladder."

"They just didn't care about competing," said Molly, knowing the excuse sounded flimsy.

"Perhaps. Still strange though, eh?" said Michael, then more forceful, "Now please, come with us."

"Okay. Can I use the restroom first? I just had two bottles of soda."

The officers exchanged glances, then Michael nodded. "Be quick."

The next moment she was in the bathroom, staring at her large bowl of GYM UP. She could go out tonight. And go out with a bang . . .

***

Five minutes later she was seated in the back of the squad car, her stomach in knots. It wasn't from nerves, it wasn't from going to prison. It was from the amount of GYM UP she'd just stuffed in her mouth. Her insides were boiling, her heart was racing and her vision was blurring.

There was a good chance she'd just committed suicide. No person on Earth had ingested so much of the magical drug.

Then, she looked down at her feet, and could feel them getting longer—could feel her toes at the edge, threatening to pop the seams. Her shoulders were pressing tightly into the fabric of her shirt, her bra about to snap in the back. Already her head was moving up, higher than the men sitting in the front seats.

"Uh . . . guys? I would advise you to pull over," she said, turning onto her side, ready to rip through the car and become a goddess.

Small Package

Emily Kruger had been delivering packages for United Parcel for almost two-weeks now and she was ready to get her first paycheck. She was behind her peers; twenty-two years old with zero college under her belt and no place to live. She still stayed with her parents, and although they'd been out of town for the past month on one of their extravagant cruises, she still longed for her independence. United Parcel was meant to be her ticket to that independence.

Luckily her run wasn't very large. She serviced the Midland area of her town, which only stretched for about twenty blocks. A lot of the people were regulars, and she became friends with the nice ones, learned the schedules and how to avoid the mean ones. Emily was a tall girl, long brown hair nearly to her ass which she kept pulled back in a hat while she worked. The packages weren't too burdensome—she stayed in shaped, spent three days a week at the local gym, so she had no problem lifting most things.

She'd often stop for a bite of lunch at her favorite burger joint and, on warm days, sit outside under the umbrella. Right across the street was Marigold University, or at least a large part of it. Emily knew very little of college life, other than when sports were concerned. She knew enough about Marigold to see that it dominated this little university town. Buildings with the MU surrounded by an orange flower seemed to be all over the place. And many of her deliveries were addressed to student dorms or professor offices.

On the evening that changed her life, she was making one such delivery, as it was addressed to the science wing of the campus, a large complex on the southern end that she'd never visited before. This was her last delivery, the heat of the day on the wane, and most of the students were tired and shuffling back toward their dorms and common areas. She tucked the package under her arm and counted doors, looking for a 106. The name on the box read Dr. Bullock, Engineering.

Around the corner, Emily had to step over painting supplies because someone had been in the middle of turning the bright green hallway into a muted, understated gray. Plastic tarps were strewn about, a couple of ladders, and an assortment of abandoned paint brushes and rollers. At the end of the hall she found 106, as it was the only door still hanging open.

Inside, she found an older man, his back to the door. He fit the classic professor look—white frizzy hair, argyle sweater, pencil behind his ear. As he moved, she could tell that he was holding something in his hand, possibly a gun. Although this gun looked like something out of *Star Wars* . . . or was it the other sci-fi one? She could never remember. He brought it up, made an adjustment, then turned to the side and pointed it at what looked like a department store female mannequin. Emily was so transfixed on what he was doing to move or say anything. And then, he pulled the trigger.

The mannequin blazed with orange light. Emily momentarily switched what she was watching to see the man, who she was now sure had to be Dr. Bullock, pull the smoking gun away and drop it at his side. A few seconds later, she joined him as an unknown observer, watching the mannequin as if something extraordinary should happen— and in a span of two heartbeats, it did.

Slowly, the mannequin began to shrink.

The plastic girl's fingers got shorter, stubbier. Her feet dragged across the floor but luckily she was standing on a metal base that, likewise, was growing smaller. Emily just stared in awe as the mannequin became half its size, then half that, and then half that. When the shrinking stopped it looked like a Barbie doll, only that wasn't quite right. A Barbie doll was a little bigger than this. This mannequin would reach Barbie's crotch.

Emily, out of pure surprise, dropped the package. The sound of it hitting startled her, and she backed up, this time slamming into a ladder and knocking a paint tray and roller to the ground where they clattered heavily. Startled a second time, Emily jumped, but so too did Dr. Bullock. He whirled around, and with his finger on the trigger, zapped the tense girl. She started to run immediately, half out of fear, half out of embarrassment. Surely she was faster than his gun, right? She didn't think the orange glow landed on her skin, but why was she suddenly feeling flush and sick to her stomach?

"Wait! Come back! I will explain everything!" Dr. Bullock called behind her. Emily was already out of earshot though—she'd already crashed through the far-end door and was making her way around the staircase, as the first floor of the science building was a floor below the ground. She didn't know why she ran—only that her fight or flight instinct kicked in and told her to fly like hell. When she made it to the exit, that's when she noticed the change.

She tripped over the doorframe as she left the building. No one was around to see it, and she was glad to be spared such embarrassment, but knew she probably needed *some*one to see her. On the ground, looking back, she watched as her feet slid out of the boots. Emily didn't care about them, just stood up and ran down the steps, her socks peeling off her sweaty feet as she stepped down.

She started toward her truck, but the cars zipping by on the highway near where she parked startled her. They looked and sounded absolutely massive, like thunder solidified. Instinctively she turned to the left and headed toward another building whose door was propped open.

Her frantic mind could no longer escape the fact that she was shrinking. The same thing that happened to the mannequin was now happening to her, and if logic followed, she would wind up the same size as the plastic girl, given that they were equally as tall in the beginning. Emily slid out of her pants, then her panties. When she was halfway across the lawn, her shirt and bra became so burdensome that she shed those as well. Now, a quickly dwindling woman was racing through the grass, and feeling no closer to the next building no matter how fast she went.

By the time she reached the step, it was almost over her head. She couldn't have been more than six or seven inches tall. The whole world looked scary, massive. Light didn't refract the same way. Colors, some standing out more and others fading into drabs that she thought was normal only to tiny eyes. Sound didn't travel as it did when she was big. It was like she'd landed on an alien planet where she had to learn how to use her body all over again. The grass was up to her waist and she was thankful the maintenance crew had cut it or else she'd be in a jungle. Emily pushed the thought of bugs and vermin out of her head.

She needed to get help. At that moment she wasn't thinking clearly. Perhaps Dr. Bullock had fired on accident, perhaps not. She felt like a dog whose owner accidently kicked it during a dark night—the dog knew there was no malice, but avoided the owner for a little while just the same. Right now, she wanted to be away from the doctor and thought this place might be her best chance to be safe.

It was an endeavor to get up the steps. She had to hop up, then lift herself, then roll onto the next one. Giant feet padded past her and she let out a tiny yelp—loud to her ears but most likely not to anyone else. She pressed her back against the edge of the steps and watched as two women walked out of the building. Next, another woman, this one talking on a cellphone entered, not paying one bit of attention to the shrunken girl on the steps. Emily couldn't help but feel her face turn red when the giantess was overhead—she was wearing as skirt, with no panties.

That pussy could swallow me whole, thought the tiny woman, not sure where that particular thought came from, but knew it turned her on just the same.

The building, while massive to her small size, was nowhere near as intimidating as the outside world. Here, there were a few people milling about, sitting on sofas, watching television, and to Emily's non-college mind, she had no idea the purpose of such a living space. Then, it clicked. This was a girls' dormitory. She'd made a delivery here once, on her second day on the job. That job now seemed over, a thought that made her incredibly sad.

She counted four girls in the middle of the room, all on sofas that formed a horseshoe around a television. They were massive, needless to say, but also quite beautiful. Two of them were lying back to back, massive feet hanging over the opposite ends of the sofa—their toes dangling impossibly high in the air. The third girl was in a recliner and the fourth was on the edge of another sofa. None of them were interested in the television, only their cellphones. Emily thought she should try to get their attention.

Her little feet padded across the hardwood floor, across a plush rug, and into the middle of their viewing area. The red-haired girl sitting on the edge of the sofa was voluminous, even at Emily's small size. Her breasts were massive, as evidenced by the way her shirt button groaned with each breath. Her nails were long as she pecked on her phone's screen. It may have been possible to get her attention—her foot was touching the floor, a massive piece of meat that was as long as Emily's current body. But no, Emily decided against that, fearful the giantess would unknowingly squash the shrunken woman.

Instead, Emily circled the massive coffee table, its legs twice the girth of her body. On one side, a stack of books had been piled up, and she easily scaled these until she was able to pull herself up onto the surface of the table. It felt so high being here, and also disorienting since the table was glass and it gave the illusion she was floating in the air. When Emily saw a soda can, which came up to her neck, the perspective of her size became clear. It was frightening to be so small. Nevertheless, she stepped upon another small stack of books and began to jump up and down while waving her hands.

One of the girls on the sofa, a beautiful blond whose hair was tied back, caught movement from the corner of her eye. She dropped her phone to the cushion, leaned in and squinted her eyes at the small, flailing woman.

"Oh my God, Jenn, are you seeing this?" The girl named Jenn, feeling the blond girl lean away, turned around, then followed her gaze to the table. Now both were watching with rapt attention. The rest of the ladies, now sensing their reverie broken, made likewise adjustments to come in close and look at the shrunken woman.

"What is it?" asked Jenn.

"She's a fairy," said the voluminous redhaired girl.

"Don't be stupid, Ariana. She doesn't have wings," said the fourth girl that Emily had barely noticed until now—a short waif with close-cropped hair. She was wearing shorts and combat boots.

"Then what do you think she is, Sabrina?" asked Jenn.

Sabrina just shrugged. "An alien?"

The girls broke into riotous laughter that put Emily to ease. That was a very good thing because she was feeling a little self-conscious having so many big, beautiful faces crowd around her. After all, she was naked.

The fourth girl, the blond with the beautifully toned physique got on her knees and approached the shrunken woman. Her arms were massive as she put them up on the table and folded them over. Looking at flesh so closely was like seeing some alien creature. The girl's eyes were blue, her lips puffy and perfect.

"I'm Amy," she said. "Do you have a name?"

"Um, I'm Emily."

The girls exchanged surprised looks, as if they weren't expecting the tiny doll to talk back.

"What are you?" asked Jenn.

"I'm a person. I'm just . . . I don't know. Shrunken down? I got zapped with a laser by some guy."

"How did you end up here?" asked Ariana.

The girls all came around to one side so Emily could address them all without having to turn circles on the table. She explained how she'd been delivering packages, had made one final delivery to the science wing of the university and was unwillingly zapped by a mad scientist's shrink ray. She told them about the mannequin, how she freaked out, how she ran, and how she was afraid of the man who'd done it.

"That's got to be Dr. Bullock," said Jenn. "He's harmless, really. But I could see how this would be scary."

"I can't be stuck this way," said Emily. "I need help."

"Should we call 911?" asked Sabrina.

"Or we can go talk to the doctor for you, if you'd like," said Amy.

Emily nodded, although she didn't want to be there for it. There was something about being shrunken down, about a *man* shrinking her down, that was somewhat infuriating and dehumanizing. For some reason, these four ladies, as varied as they could be, made her feel comfortable.

"Are you hungry?" asked Ariana.

Emily shook her head, subconsciously covering her nakedness.

"Listen," said Sabrina, blowing the hair out of her face. "Jenn and I share a dorm. How would you like to come upstairs with us and we'll see if we can't find you something to wear?"

Emily nodded, not sure what else to do.

Sabrina looked over to Jenn who just nodded. Jenn was the posh one of the group—this ragtag group of friends was the proverbial *Spice Girls* of college life. It took Emily a moment to place Jenn's skirt, and to realize this was the underwear-free woman who'd walked into the dorm house just before Emily had climbed up the steps herself.

A warm hand wrapped around her shivering little body and lifted her into the air. Emily felt a sudden rush of vertigo but it quickly passed as the giantess moved out of the common area and up the steps. Emily couldn't help but look up at her and lick her lips—she loved beautiful women, and to see one so large and up so close, was a little intoxicating. She only hoped she'd be dropped before the one carrying her felt a warm stickiness.

Sabrina and Jenn's dorm room was at the far end of the hall. It was spacious, but Emily knew that was an illusion because this place, in truth, was probably a shoebox. There was a queen bed, but that wasn't quite right either because there was a small, barely noticeable crease in the comforter. It was two twin beds pushed together. Did that mean these girls slept together? The idea of that was also intoxicating.

Jenn placed her on the nightstand next to a lamp that towered over her. The light beneath the shade was so bright that it hurt her eyes, but luckily her giant caretaker noticed her dismay and quickly turned it off. Sabrina pulled the door shut and then both girls sat on the bed, watching their new little friend.

"Is there anyone we should call?" asked Jenn.

Emily shook her head. "My parents are out of town. I guess the only people who would be concerned right now is United Parcel. They'll miss their truck, at least."

"We'll take care of it," said Sabrina.

"Why are you two being so nice to me?" asked Emily.

"We just figure you've been through a lot today. It must be scary," said Jenn.

"It is. But I guess I'm getting used to it. Things aren't looking as scary. At least not here."

Sabrina said, "It's good to talk. Let's get to know each other, shall we?"

And for the next few hours, that's what they did. Sabrina managed to find a piece of fabric which she stapled together to create a robe for the tiny woman. It wasn't the most comfortable, certainly not the prettiest, but it kept her from being naked.

Sabrina talked about her parents down in Alabama, her dog Scooter, and her brother who just graduated high school. Jenn talked about the golf course her dad owned, how she'd never been allowed to have friends growing up, and how she felt she was socially inept when it came to talking to and meeting new people. At some point during the evening, one of the girls must have taken a break from texting long enough to order a pizza because a delivery guy dropped off three medium pies while Emily hid behind the lamp. Amy and Ariana also came over to eat, and the four girls formed a circle on the bed, with the pizza and Emily in the middle.

She had trouble eating, even with the help of Amy who took a plastic knife and cut the pizza into tiny slivers. Cheese and pepperoni were tough to chew at her small size, but the bread and sauce were just fine. Food tasted odd being so little—she could imagine a dozen different reasons why this could be, but either way, it didn't make eating any more enjoyable. She ate just enough to keep the rumble in her stomach away.

"We didn't see Bullock," said Ariana. "He must have gone home already. Last class is around four o'clock anyway, so it makes sense."

Amy nodded and added, "We did find your clothes. You left a trail all the way here. I took your keys out of your pocket and pulled your truck into the university parking lot. It'll be safer here."

"Thank you," said Emily. "You guys are really sweet."

Sometime later, after Ariana and Amy went over to their dorm, Jenn presented Emily with a shoebox filled with socks. As the shrunken girl surveyed the contents, she looked up at the giantess and wondered the reason she was being shown such a thing.

"They're clean," said Jenn, mistaking the girl's lack of understanding for reluctance. "It's for you. A bed."

"Oh," said Emily, finally catching on.

Jenn placed it next to the lamp and said, "C'mon. This won't be pleasant, but I'm sure you need it."

"What?" asked the tiny woman.

"I'm going to take you to the sink so you can . . . do your business."

"Thank you," said Emily. She'd needed to use the bathroom all evening but was holding it because she didn't feel confident enough to tell the others.

"Do you want a shower? I can turn the water on and leave you a dollop of soap or bath wash."

"Maybe in the morning," said Emily. "I'm exhausted. This has been a trying day. I think I'd just rather go on to bed."

After she did her business in the sink, to which Jenn cleaned away without even looking, the giant woman took her back to the bedroom and placed her in the box of lumpy socks. It felt amazing on her skin, and even though the fabric hid the scent of the giantess's smell, Emily was still small enough to detect it. The scent of Jenn's (and possibly Sabrina's) feet made her heart race.

When Emily finally did slip off, she remarked that the girls did in fact sleep together. Jenn was already on her side, facing away from the shoebox and the shrunken woman. Sabrina sat awake reading a book by the soft glow of a nightlight clipped to her headboard. It was a peaceful way to live, but she still hoped it wouldn't be forever.

Sometime during the night she woke to a screech.

When she sat up, she looked around the room, her eyes focusing in the darkness. The girls had a small television that was showing some late-night golf tournament footage, but it was enough light to cast on the bed. Emily didn't see anything but a mound—no hair, no arms, no legs. Only a moving, writhing lump under the covers. But as she watched, the blanket flew black, and there was Jenn, mouth open in pure ecstasy, hands in her hair. Sabrina couldn't be seen, but Emily knew she was under the covers, working her girlfriend over, and over quite well if Jenn's face was to be believed.

Emily felt a tingle between her own legs at the sight of the two giant women fucking. She brought a hand down, surprised by how wet she'd become. Using the socks as a pillow, she propped them up so she could lean back and watch the show. Her fingers did circles around her clit, and as the women moaned, so did she. As Jenn shuddered in the throes of her orgasm, the girls changed positions, and when they did, Sabrina, hair a mess, looked over and saw the shrunken woman pleasing herself.

"Oh, God, Jenn, look!"

Jenn came out of her post-orgasm stupor and found the shrunken woman. Emily didn't care. She was so turned on, so worked up to watch something she'd only dreamed about. She loved women, but had never experimented with any. Now, seeing it performed as if on the big screen at a theater was more than she could handle.

"Want to watch a little closer?" asked Sabrina.

Emily just nodded.

The giantess scooped up the small girl and placed her on the edge of the bed. Meanwhile, Jenn had attached a rather long, pink dildo and was getting into position by the headboard. Sabrina bent over, doggie-style position, and her eyes were locked on the small girl. Emily knew the exact moment of penetration, could see the girl's eyes flutter, could see her face acknowledge pain and then sweet, sweet pleasure. Emily kept fingering herself, watching the giant woman's face move close and then retreat with each pounding of the faux dick.

Just when Emily thought she may come, Sabrina grabbed her by the legs and pulled her forward. Emily made a little yipping sound, mostly out of surprise, but she didn't have long to question it because a large tongue suddenly found her sweet spot—it was warm, wet, and the scent of Jenn was still on her breath. Emily just lay there, feeling worked over by a machine rather than a person. When she finally did cum, the giant lady lapped it up, then kissed her. Then, Sabrina put her cheek to the bed, closed her eyes and smiled while Jenn finished.

Afterwards, they talked for a little bit and then went back to sleep. Emily looked across the room to Sabrina, who was grinning ear to ear. Jenn never even realized their little tryst had become something of a three-way.

***

When she woke next morning, feeling more relaxed than she had in months, with the light streaming in through the curtains, she felt as though she were being watched. Normally she didn't care, and her mind quickly shifted gears to remembering that she'd been shrunken down and had made friends with a few incredibly awesome women. But when she opened her eyes, those four awesome women were to the rear of the room, while a scraggily-bearded man with unkempt white hair examined her.

Emily quickly pulled a sock up to her body, using it as a mini-sheet. The man, now who she recognized to be Dr. Bullock, smiled at her attempt at modesty. He wasn't mean, there was no malice there. In half a heartbeat she went from wanting to scream to carefully backing up, trying to understand what he was doing.

"How do you feel?" he asked her, his voice coming out strong, despite his age.

"Fine. It's just . . . weird."

"I would imagine so," he agreed. "Congratulations. You're the first human test subject to undergo being shrunken down."

"Why did you do this?" she asked.

"I didn't mean to," he said, face breaking down a little. "You startled me, is all. I tried to chase after you but you were gone. I looked around campus for an hour."

"You could've followed her clothes, dude," said Amy. She was wearing tight leggings and running shoes, as if she'd just come from the gym. A fine sheen of sweat covered her face and neck.

"I didn't see the clothes. I barely recognized that it was a woman before she ran off. I was too busy looking for a tiny human. Because I knew that's what she'd be."

"So can you fix me?" asked Emily, standing up but using one of the socks to cover her body. The fabric skirt had been shed through the night.

His face darkened a little, and just when Emily thought she'd be driven into full-panic mode, he answered, "You don't need me to fix you. You are already fixing yourself."

"What does that mean?" asked Ariana.

"It means she will grow back on her own. The shrinking effect isn't permanent."

"That's great news!" said Emily.

"Uh huh," said Dr. Bullock. "But it will take about a month."

"So . . . she's stuck this way?" Sabrina asked.

"Temporarily," he affirmed. "I would love to keep a check on you, if that's alright. This is amazing science, after all."

"I . . . guess so," she said, feeling a little deflated by the news.

"Don't worry, Emily, we will take good care of you," said Ariana.

"We don't mind. You can stay here with us until you're big again," Jenn added.

"This would be smart," said Dr. Bullock. "I'll come by every so often and check on you. This is quite remarkable."

"But . . . I don't know how I can just uproot my life like this," said Emily.

"You don't have much choice, dear," said Bullock. "It's either here or, if I were to announce my device to the world, most likely in a lab under much different conditions. Take these girls up on their offer. It might be fun."

"It definitely will be," said Sabrina, with a wink.

Bullock added, "These girls tell me you make delivers for United Parcel. I know the regional manager. I'll contact her, tell her you are . . . under doctor's care, and that someone should come claim their truck. That should take care of your job until you're large again."

"Thank you," said Emily. Quite frankly, she was more worried about her job than anything else. Bullock's words put her at ease.

"Okay then," he said, standing up. "I'll be in touch. Girls, keep her away from cats if you have any."

***

The next week went by smoothly with Emily continuing to live in Sabrina and Jenn's dorm room, sleeping in the shoebox, bathing and relieving herself (at opposite times) in the sink. She'd once grown brave enough to shower with the giant women, which turned out to be one of the sexiest experiences of her life. Looking up at those towering, sudsy women in all their curvaceous glory, knowing she could literally be stepped on, was something of a turn on she'd never known.

It didn't take long for their relationship to become overly sexual. Emily was the right size to be passed around between the women. She served as a human dildo for both Sabrina and Jenn—sometimes letting the girls scissor around her tiny body. There weren't many nights that Emily went to bed where she wasn't covered in the girls' scent.

Amy and Ariana's dorm room was right across the hall, and since there was no reason for anyone to come to the four girls' floor, they kept their door open at all times so that Emily could move about however she wanted. They'd erected little ladders and ramps up to the high places, placed Emily's cellphone on a permanent charger so she could text (something that was comical at her small size) whenever she needed someone to help her.

One morning Emily found herself walking across the hall to the other girls' room. Most everyone had classes that morning but Amy didn't until around noon, three days a week. She took that opportunity to get a run in. Emily wasn't much of a fitness buff, certainly not to the degree of Amy, but she knew the campus circuit in which the fit girl ran was at least four miles. The very thought made Emily's head swim.

When Emily entered, she could feel the steam billowing out of the shower. Just by the door, Amy had kicked off her running shoes and clothes, then apparently bounded naked across the room and into the bathroom. Seeing that large pile of sweaty clothes made Emily's heart race. She couldn't help but walk up to it, smelling Amy's scent all over. The shrunken woman burrowed under the garments, feeling the warm, sticky sweat of her friend. A strong scent emanated from the socks, turned inside out, and the shoes.

She took one of the socks, pressed her face into the fabric and breathed. The giantess's scent was all over it. Emily didn't know why this was such a turn on—she actually felt like a bit of a freak for it, but she didn't care. The scent that came off a sexy woman's foot was delectable. She leaned against the shoe and wrapped her arms around the sock.

Eventually she righted the shoe, then hopped inside, as if sitting in a canoe. The pad was wet with Amy's sweat and she found herself flipping around and burrowing toward the far end. She could feel the giantess's heat still around the indention of the toes, and she just lay there, feeling very much in heaven. This behavior was never a part of her when she was big, so she wondered if the shrink ray had caused some sort of nymphomaniac to rise to the surface.

Suddenly, fingers grasped her legs and pulled her out, dangling her upside down. Amy deposited the shrunken woman on her palm and looked down at her. The giantess's hair was up in a towel, her skin moist and glistening. The heat coming from her was intoxicating and she couldn't help but smile up at her.

"Got a thing for feet, do you?" asked the giantess.

Emily shrugged, but she was smiling nonetheless.

"Good, then you can help me with a job."

***

For the next hour, Amy and Emily chatted about all things—life, love, school, work, and friends. The whole time it happened, Emily used a brush to paint the giantess's toenails a brilliant shade of pink. It was a fun job, but the acrylic was so strong she often needed to stopper the bottle and walk away to catch her breath.

"So I've heard you've been having a little bit of . . . fun next door," said Amy, running a comb through her thick hair.

Emily grinned, putting a long line of pink across the giantess's big toe. "It's been interesting."

"Jenn and I used to fuck," said Amy, longingly. "Before Sabrina came into the picture."

"So they're pretty serious then?" asked Emily.

"I don't think it's that. I just took a step back in case they wanted to, you know, make it something real?"

"I get that. I'm sure you girls could still have fun if you wanted."

"Maybe," Amy said, a little dismissively. "So what's it like? Being shrunken down?"

"It's not so bad. Let's me be creative, that's for sure."

"Sounds incredibly fun." Emily didn't know if it was subconscious or not, but when Amy shifted her weight to adjust her foot, the towel loosened and her wet pussy was on full display. It looked so good, so inviting, especially after Emily had already gotten a taste of one specific scent.

Amy followed the shrunken woman's eyes down and smiled. "Like what you see, little lady?"

Emily stood up, stoppered the nail polish and nodded.

Amy pulled the whole towel back, completely showing the shrunken woman her nude, glistening body. She took the bottle of polish and put it aside, then positioned herself so that she was facing the little woman more directly. She brought fingers down to her thighs, rubbed her legs a little, then held herself slightly open.

"Do you want to?" she asked Emily. "Do you want to go in me?"

Emily, as if in a stupor, only nodded. She walked up to the giant pussy, put a hand up, felt it quiver. She brought her face to it and licked, coming away a little sticky. Amy was ready to get started, had probably thought about it the moment she came out of the bathroom and found the tiny woman moving around in her shoe.

Emily wasted no time pushing her way into the woman. Amy's back arched and she grabbed at the pillows but she kept her lower half steady as not to unsettle the shrunken woman. When Emily had trouble pushing through, Amy took two fingers and gently shoved her. It didn't take long for the giantess to become fully wet, and Emily had trouble finding her footing within the woman's slick pussy. It was so inviting here—so warm, wet, and tight. She was like a giant blanket.

Amy was one of the fastest girls to get off. No sooner had she started to push on the vagina walls and spin around did a giant gush wash over her. There was barely any time to revel in a job well down because fingers immediately entered the dark, wet cave and snatched her out. She was expecting to look up into the satisfied eyes of Amy but these were green, not blue.

It wasn't Amy who was holding her, but Ariana.

The redheaded buxom beauty licked the shrunken girl from head to toe, then laid back and deposited Emily on her stomach. She started to unbutton her shirt, not saying a word, only looking down at the tiny doll in a seductive way.

"You know you just fucked my girlfriend," said Ariana playfully. "You have to make us even now."

When Ariana's shirt was unbuttoned, she pulled up her bra and then picked up Emily so she could one-handedly take them off. As she settled back against the pillow, she dropped the shrunken woman on her massive breast, the nipple rising to meet her. Amy just watched, a hand going down below to keep things warm.

Emily worked her breast until she was relieved by the other giantess who simply pushed her south. Emily took this as a sign to get busy so while she was inside her second pussy of the day, she took the opportunity to finger herself and lick the juices of a new friend. Every so often, Ariana's lips would part, light would come in, and for a brief moment, she would catch Amy's tongue, invitingly close to the tiny woman's body.

Later, as Emily lay on the bed between the giantesses' feet, she didn't think life could get any better than this. Now, if only she could get all four of them together at once . . .

***

The girls were very good to her. After only a few days in their care, they found an old dollhouse at a yard sale and brought it home to Amy and Ariana's room. It was spacious enough to be like a real house and that sense of normalcy made Emily feel much better. They'd even purchased doll furniture, clothes, and a bed that wasn't a shoebox. She routinely asked if Amy would leave a sweaty sock for her to cozy up to when she wasn't around.

Bullock came around every few days and never stayed long. He asked Emily basic questions such as how was her diet, was she ever too hot or too cold, and did her bowels move normally. Emily tried to answer these questions as best she could but felt he was never quite satisfied with her answers. Still, he gave her privacy on most days.

About two weeks after she'd been shrunk, she made a discovery.

While serving as a human fucktoy for Sabrina, something she did almost every other day since she'd become a very willing party favor for the girls, she realized she couldn't move about as freely as before. It didn't occur to her until later that night, while falling asleep in the doll bed and her feet were hanging over the edge.

"I'm growing back," she said the next morning. Jenn had poured her a thimble full of coffee.

"Are you sure?" she asked.

"Definitely. I'm not going to be a good fucktoy for much longer."

And so she wasn't.

Two weeks later and she was nearly ten inches tall. She could still fit half her body inside the girls, but it wasn't nearly as fun for them. However, it was increasingly more pleasurable for *her*. She'd stumbled upon the magic size . . . the sweetest height for a giant tongue to hit all the right spots. It would be interesting to see how sex would change as she added inches.

A couple days later Amy came in from class while they all watched television in the common room. Sabrina or Jenn often kept Emily hidden, tucked away between their legs or down in the cushions next to them. No other girls living in the building (not that there were many) knew about the shrunken girl. Amy walked with a determination that the whole group found odd, and as a result, stopped talking, texting, and looked up.

"Got a minute guys? I wanna talk to you all." Without waiting around, she headed up the steps and out of sight.

Sabrina picked up Emily and followed behind Ariana and Jenn. Amy was sitting on the edge of her bed, her backpack across her lap. She pulled out a small wooden box and flipped the lid open.

Inside laid the shrink ray.

"What is that?" asked Sabrina.

"It's the shrink ray," said Emily. "How did you get this?"

"He's out of town. My friend takes his class and said he went to Michigan to visit his sister. Won't be back for two weeks."

"And why do you have it?" asked Ariana.

Amy took a breath, turned the gun so that the handle and trigger faced the group. "I want you to shrink me."

"What?" more than one voice said at once.

"I've been turning it over in my brain and I think it would be fun. You're all losing your shrunken fucktoy anyway. Let me take over."

"Are you crazy?" asked Ariana. "You can't just uproot your life that way."

Amy shook her head. "I'm not uprooting anything. I took my last final this morning and my next classes don't start for another three weeks. That last week I'll probably be big enough to still go." She shrugged, laughed to herself, and added, "I'll just wear heels."

"You're crazy," said Sabrina.

"Nah. I just wanna get played with. Will you let me?" She spoke to the whole group, but was looking up at Jenn.

They each nodded.

Amy looked down at Emily and said, "Care to have a roommate?"

Emily just nodded, thinking the girl crazy for even attempting this.

"Will you do the honors?" Amy asked Jenn, holding the shrink ray out.

She took it, silently, looking down at the device as if it were the oddest thing she'd ever held.

"Do I just point and shoot?" she asked, looking to first to Amy and then to Emily for an answer. Both girls just shrugged.

"Probably," said Amy finally, not wanting the question to hang unanswered.

"Okay. Are you ready?"

Amy stood up, held her arms down at her sides. "No, wait!" She said, frantically waving her arms to stop the girl. "Emily, how long does it take? You know, to shrink?"

"Just a few minutes. It's fast. You only have about two or three minutes before you're tiny."

She started to undress, undoing her belt and finally dropping her pants in the floor until she stood there looking like *Winnie the Pooh*.

"Now what are you doing?" asked Ariana.

Amy came up to her, gave her a kiss on the lips, the last normal one they'd share for a month. "After she zaps me, I want you to go down on me until I'm tiny."

Without a word, she nodded, licked her lips, and waited.

Jenn lined up the shot and then a collective gasp ran through the room as the gun expelled a blast of orange energy and then disappeared just as fast. She laid the smoking gun on the nightstand and watched as Ariana threw her girlfriend down, quickly kissed beneath her shirt and then found the sweet spot.

It was incredibly hot watching the women go at it. Amy put her feet up on Ariana's shoulders, squeezed her head with powerful thighs. But then, they were diminishing. Emily watched as the toes crept smaller, feet sliding off, and then her little legs were in the air where they continued to dwindle away. Amy's voice stayed the same pitch, only getting lower, as if the volume on a radio was being turned down. By the time the shrinking was over, none of them could see her—only Ariana's head bobbing up and down as she licked the tiny woman from head to toe.

She finally held up Amy for the room to see, a shrunken woman just like Emily. Well, almost like Emily. When Ariana placed her next to the other shrunken woman, there was a marked difference. Amy barely came up to Emily's belly button. Just a couple of weeks ago, this was how small Emily had been.

This turn of events became fun for the whole group. It was just as much fun for Amy and Emily to have sex with each other as it was with the big people. Emily's fingers were massive to the tiny woman's pussy, so she used them to great effect. Sabrina had a kink for watching the small women fuck on her stomach, so they did that while Jenn went down on her. It was all so surreal yet so incredibly hot.

Amy also had a thing for feet, so they spent many nights under the soles of the giant caretakers. On more than one night they would each take a foot, usually from Sabrina, and massage while she watched television.

Amy and Emily never seemed to change sizes to each other because they were both slowly, minutely, growing back at the same rate. However, Emily noticed a huge difference in the world around her and especially the other women. In another week, she was double her size, now standing at over a foot tall. This size was fun, but she was losing the ability to get her face inside the women. In another few days she'd only be able to fuck them with arms and legs.

When Amy asked Ariana to return the shrink ray to Bullock's office, she returned a few hours later and said it couldn't be done. While he was out of town, his place had been locked down, so for now, they would keep it safe and hidden.

Three weeks into the shrinking and Emily was the size of a child. She could take care of herself now, sleep in a normal bed, use the toilet, fix her own food. Amy was still less than half her size and it was fun pressing her face into Emily's waiting pussy. The shrunken woman got her off more efficiently than the rest.

When Emily was nearly level with Ariana's massive breasts, Sabrina came running in, a look of pure panic and worry in her face.

"What? What's wrong?" asked Jenn.

"You all haven't heard, have you?" she asked.

"Heard what?" Emily asked.

"Dr. Bullock was killed in a car wreck on his way home from his sisters. There's a sub teacher in there now."

"God, how awful," said Amy.

"You guys," said Sabrina. "What do we do with the shrink ray?"

Amy and Emily looked at each other and shrugged, then Amy said, "I don't think anyone knows about it."

"You really don't think so?" Jenn asked. "This was a major discovery for science. Surely he told someone. A colleague, his sister?"

Amy shook her head. "In the times we talked after he started coming to visit Emily he acted like no one knew about it. Like he was embarrassed to tell people."

Jenn half-smiled, her mouth showing teeth. "So . . . then it basically belongs to us now, right?"

The girls just looked at each other, no one wanting to admit it, but that seemed to be the way of things, even if a horrible tragedy delivered this wonderful device to them.

"What does this mean?" asked Ariana.

Sabrina, her face turning a dark shade of red, raised her hand and said, "It means I'm next!"

The
Dollhouse
Maker

Ashley wasn't a big fan of the German food but she was certainly glad of the pay raise her bosses had given her when she decided to make the move. Not only that, they also made sure she had above adequate housing and amenities that most people working at her firm could only dream of earning. She'd do a six-month rotation in Europe, after which she'd go back to the home office in Philadelphia. And when she did return, she'd be making almost six-figures and would have a wonderful spread on her next résumé.

Her little one-story house was little more than a bed and breakfast, but she hardly stayed there. She split her time either at work, milling over data from her company's research wing, or perusing the town just to the south. It was called Kurtz, and it was situated just a few miles from the city of Hamburg. Kurtz was picturesque; all the things the magazine and travel brochures would like you to believe about German hospitality. The cottages were thatched, the streets cobblestone, the church steeples . . . well, steep. She'd never been in any place like this before, and the beauty of it helped to make her homesickness wane a little.

She had no friends here, but that was okay. Ashley was more of an introvert, anyway. No, that wasn't quite right either. As her last boyfriend had told her, she wasn't so much of an introvert as she was a loner. He'd meant it to be an insult—why, the guy had broken up with her two weeks later—but she didn't take it that way. She was very much a loner, and that was perfectly fine with her. She didn't need anyone. If Ashley got lonely, she had the internet and her social media. If she got horny, she had her big bag of toys stuffed beneath the armoire in her bedroom.

One of the things she liked most about Kurtz was that main street was lined with quaint little shops that looked like they'd been hand drawn from a *Disney* cartoon.

The buildings were uniform, brownstone, stucco, and brick, and they went on for at least half a mile. Even though the town was small, the streets were often bustling till well after dark, and even then they barely emptied. The type of people simply changed. In the day, those who needed to shop. At night, those who wanted to date or grab a cup of coffee.

One of her favorite shops was the bookstore—a three-story building with a colorful placard reading the name—something Ashley would never have been capable—swinging in the slight wind. She could spend hours here, and often did on the days she wasn't needed at work. Ashley would buy her coffee (a cinnamon dolce with skim milk) two doors down, then bring it to the bookstore and get lost in a story. She often fancied herself in those tales—stories like *Beauty and the Beast* and *Alice in Wonderland*. The stories where the characters could take their time and learn their surroundings. She didn't feel that way in her real life, often rushed to get her work done. Those days in the bookstore were hers, when life was allowed to slow. She didn't think it could ever get any better than this.

Until she found the dollhouse store.

She'd passed it by many times. It was situated just between the little general store where she bought milk and bread, and the coffee shop. It didn't interest her, but then again, why should it? Ashley was not a child, she was a woman of twenty-four years. There was no reason why she would want a dollhouse or any of the accompanying accessories no matter how lovely they looked, seated in the foreground of a whimsy diorama. But one day, as she was walking by to reach the coffee shop, the window dressing caught her eye. She passed up the whole store, then quickly backtracked, drawn to the display on the other side of the glass.

It was a tiny neighborhood, built with little houses and props. Whoever had created this poured so much time into the details. The homes, the cars, the people—they all looked almost real-to-life, had they not been so small. Upon closer inspection Ashley noticed it was all carved of wood, but the craftsmanship was unbelievable. Someone had painstakingly created tilework in the rooms of the homes, had chiseled granite stones for the walkway, had put treads on the cars' tires—the cars themselves were metal and looked waxed to perfection. It was all so wonderfully whimsical, and Ashley found herself turning the knob and entering the store.

A tiny bell above the door announced her entry. There was no one else in the surprisingly spacious store. Then again, perhaps it was because every single piece of inventory was miniature. Most of what the store carried was mass-produced dollhouse accessories. These items were on pegboards that surrounded the shop. However, many of the displays that caught Ashley's attention were one-of-a-kind. While this store probably catered to the everyday kid who wanted a new toilet for her dollhouse's bathroom, the specialty items were clearly meant for the discerning clientele.

Dominating the center of the room was a floor display—a gothic dollhouse whose top spire nearly touched the ceiling. The home was meant to accommodate dolls no more than six-inches tall, but one would never assume such from looking outside. Like most other dollhouses, this one hinged open in the center, spreading apart so someone could get to the rooms—and inside this one, there were many. Not only that, each room was carefully decorated. Ashley leaned in close just to appreciate the detail.

In the main foyer, a chandelier hung from a frescoed ceiling. The crystals in the chandelier were so intricate that she wondered how any man or machine could carve them so. On the walls hung portraits, also incredibly detailed. She could say the same thing for the furniture—thick, stout chairs and sofas on wooden legs, adorned with cushions and pillows that Ashley was sure looked stitched.

Her fingernail tapped the shiny toilet, sure it would make a dull, plastic thud, but in truth dinged as if made of real porcelain. Even the tiny seat moved up and down on a hinge that must have been almost microscopic because as much as she squinted, she couldn't see it. Everything in this room and all the others held a detail that she didn't think was possible.

Ashley looked around the rest of the store. Many of the smaller displays held various pieces of doll furniture. Shelves of tables, chairs, armoires, beds, cabinets, mirrors, throw rugs, and lamps were all immaculately placed and polished, holding the same detail as the rooms and furniture in the middle dollhouse. She loved manipulating the moveable parts—the drawers, the handles, the buttons—they were just like normal-sized things, scaled down as if by magic.

"Can I bag that for you?" asked a voice behind Ashley.

She whirled around to see a raven-haired woman standing behind the counter, having appeared from the doorway to the back. Ashley thought she was beautiful—tall, slender, with delicate hands she'd placed upon the glass counter holding little pieces of jewelry. A thin sheen of sweat covered her face, as if she'd been working, and a greasy smock hung across her narrow shoulders.

"Um, no, I'm just looking," said Ashley. "Beautiful work."

The girl beamed—she was probably around Ashley's age which brought the question of who could possibly own the dollhouse shop. She looked entirely too young to own and operate this place herself, but then again the town of Kurtz seemed to be full of young entrepreneurs. The coffeehouse, for example, was owned by a married couple in their twenties.

"Thank you," she said. Her accent was German but she spoke such good English that it was lost to the words. "All created right here." She drummed her knuckles on the counter.

"So you . . . carve these things?" Ashley asked, picking up a small desk and holding it on her hand. It looked odd, but she couldn't place the reason why.

"I do, yeah," she said. "That piece is one of my favorites." She'd come from behind the counter and approached Ashley—the woman was tall, although not eye-level. Ashley could look down at her dark hair and see the tightly pulled knot she'd tied in the back.

"They must take forever. The detail is amazing."

"They surely do. And the price reflects that, aye?" She took it from Ashley's hand, and for a moment they were touching flesh to flesh. They shared a look, but Ashley quickly averted her gaze, thinking the woman was cute but not knowing how to keep the awkwardness out of her stare.

"My, those *are* pricy," said Ashley, looking at the tag hanging from the desk's top drawer. These things cost as much as their normal-sized counterparts.

"I have lots of bills," said the girl, laughing, but firm enough for Ashley to tell she'd often been put in a position to defend her prices. Still, Ashley thought they were worth every penny.

She picked up a tiny piano and was amazed to hear it played when each of the tiny strings were struck. "This is unreal," she said, zipping her finger across it in a melodic crescendo. The girl just giggled, rocked back on her heels with her hands behind her back.

Ashley had a musical background. She'd played piano in high school, in her church, and later in college. At one time, she'd played in front of over a thousand people. She was good—once upon a time—but now she probably couldn't play one even if she tried. That was a lifetime ago. Still, she loved this little piano because it reminded her of the one back in her college's student union, the one she'd play late at night when everyone was upstairs and couldn't hear her practice.

"You really like that one, huh?" said the girl.

"I do. It's gorgeous."

"How about . . . I knock off half? It's been here for a couple of years and I'd much rather it be somewhere that it can be appreciated."

Ashley thought for a moment. Half price was still way more than she ever dreamed of spending on doll furniture—especially since this whole concept felt very childish to her. But the piano didn't have to be 'doll furniture' per se. This would look gorgeous sitting on her bookshelf or dresser. The piano was such a symbol of her personality for so long that it fit the décor of her lifestyle.

"Okay, I'll take it," she said. "I absolutely love it."

"Great," said the girl. "Let's just get it boxed up for you."

While Ashley patiently waited by the counter, she looked around and noticed for the first time the shelves went almost to the ceiling, and each one was packed with miniature furniture. It must have taken a lifetime to carve each of these things and attach the metal and plastic bits to make them seem real. Ashley tried to see into the back room and only caught a glimpse of a large piece of machinery before the woman slid in front of her to place the piano into a padded wooden box.

Ashley slid her card to pay and then the girl placed the box in a bag. As she was handing the receipt across the counter, Ashley said, "What's your name?"

The girl seemed taken aback, but smiled warmly, as if this had been the first time someone had cared to know. "I'm Clara."

"Ashley. It's very nice to meet you."

And that was the day they struck up their first conversation and started down the path to friendship. Clara was a sweet girl, shy at first, but completely opened up to Ashley the more they spoke.

Ashley was able to go to Clara's shop twice a week, and that became the spot where she drank her coffee. She much preferred this strange, beautiful German girl to the books. Clara lived alone, in the apartment above the shop. She told Ashley that her father owned the place, but went to stay in an assisted living facility a few years ago when his dementia became dangerous to others and to himself. He'd left Clara the whole business.

"So you both are dollhouse makers?" Ashley said one day over coffee. Clara had grown increasingly more flirty as the days went on, not having any friends, not having a significant other, and somehow trying to make Ashley become both. That was fine because Ashley felt the same—it had been hard to move to Germany and uproot all that she'd known. Clara was a safety net and she was thankful to have met her.

"He was. I'm more of a . . . painter and designer, I guess."

"You must have steady hands," said Ashley. She reached out and took Clara's in her own, stroking her thumbs across them.

"I suppose I do," she said. Clara rarely talked about the craft—the art of making miniature things. It was a great interest to Ashley but she could never get her friend to open up about it. At first she thought Clara was simply protecting trade secrets, but the more she talked to her, and the more she studied the little piano at home, the more she realized something wasn't quite right.

***

Ashley had placed the piano across her desk and used her magnifying lamp to see it up close. The piano was a Baldwin—a fancy brand—and just like all Baldwins, the serial number was etched along the rear right leg. She could barely see it, even under magnification, but the digits were there. The piano was detailed, but to etch the very serial number into the wood? And how could someone manage that? The whole serial number wasn't even a millimeter wide. Ashley wasn't so sure that was possible by hand *or* computer.

But the oddest thing about the piano was how it stayed relatively in tune. She'd learned enough about music theory to understand how sound was produced, and she knew that a piano with strings this small, should have a wider octave than a normal sized one. It just seemed impossible that an instrument this small would have keys that could maintain tune.

The next day, she entered the shop to find Clara behind the counter, using a pair of tweezers to set a miniature grandfather clock. When she saw Ashley enter, she looked up, smiled, then dutifully returned to her work. Ashley had her arms crossed over, wanting to confront Clara but wasn't sure why she needed to do it. So what if Clara possessed some sort of magic? Did it really matter that much? Would their friendship, possible courtship, hinge upon something so superficial?

"You okay?" asked Clara, looking up again when she felt Ashley's presence lingering over her.

"Tell me how you do it," said Ashley.

Clara froze, stood up and faced her friend. "How I do what?"

"I don't know how you make this stuff, but it's not from carving." Ashley went on to explain the discovery she'd made with the piano while Clara simply sat there and listened. Halfway through unloading, Ashley began to wonder if this was such a good idea. She didn't want to lose the only friend she'd made so far in Germany.

After a moment of stunned silence, Ashley didn't think her friend was going to open up, but finally the dollhouse maker smiled and said, "Alright, Ash. Alright. We've talked enough for me to trust you. I'll show you how I do it. Come on."

She pulled the Dutch door back and allowed Ashley to walk to the backroom, the one place in the last couple of months she'd never asked to see. That was Clara's private room, just like the upstairs, and she respected that. As soon as Ashley was standing in the back, Clara moved to the front of the store where she flipped the OPEN sign to CLOSED and deftly locked the door.

In the backroom Ashley found mostly what she'd expected. It was a spacious storage area, lined floor to ceiling with boxes and crates. At the rear hung a metal, rolling door where she guessed Clara received deliveries. The workbenches weren't what she'd expected—nothing for creating small, doll-sized furniture and houses. However, in the corner was an antique writing desk, normal-sized, and it was surrounded by tools and buckets of paint and varnish, as if Clara had been in the middle of restoring it just before Ashley had come in.

"What I'm about to show you cannot leave this room," said Clara as she entered. She started clearing away the buckets around the desk and placing the tools on their respective hooks along the walls.

"Your trade secret is that big of a deal?" asked Ashley, watching the woman shove the desk, which was on wheels, to the center of the room.

"I guess you could say that. See my dad's dad worked for Ingelstat, an engineering lab in Berlin. They started to develop . . . something. The funding fell through, the lab shut down, but my dad stored all of grandpa's things in the attic. Well one day, dad was fishing around up there and found something rather unique."

She'd unlocked a drawer beneath the counter of her workbench and pulled out a long, metal box. This she also unlocked, and nestled inside, upon a velvet lining, laid a device that looked to Ashley like a pistol, only this pistol was fitted with all sorts of weird gizmos. Along one side was a series of coils and wires, and on the other side a holster holding a cellphone. Clara struck a button and the little gun vibrated and the screen flared to life.

"Back up," she told Ashley, who promptly obeyed. Clara circled around the desk, punching in numbers on the touchscreen, producing audible beeps. When the tone changed to something Ashley assumed meant 'accepted', Clara held the gun out at arm's length toward the desk and pulled the trigger.

Not much happened, although Ashley did see a little wisp of white leave the barrel of the gun. It reminded her of fog on a cold winter morning, but this fog didn't dissipate as soon as it hit the air—this fog traveled and landed against the desk before it fizzled out. And surely that's what had happened because Ashley couldn't tell that anything else had happened. What was this strange gun? Did it paint things for her? Was it some high-tech glue gun? All of these thoughts went away when she heard the noise—a weird scraping that she couldn't place at first, but felt right away. The floor was vibrating a little because the desk's legs were dragging across it.

Miraculously before her eyes, the desk was shrinking.

Ashley was flabbergasted to see it dwindle away. The sound was deafening because it was dragging toward the center as it grew smaller and smaller. In only thirty seconds the whole thing was half its size, and in another thirty, half that. It wasn't until they were standing over it, watching it slide into its final size did it stop, now a mere five inches wide. Ashley's foot right next to it was a couple inches longer.

"Oh, God," she said, putting her hands to her face. It was making heat rush to her skin and she didn't understand why. Something about this was . . . arousing.

"Go on, you can pick it up," said Clara. "It's the same thing as it was before, only smaller."

Ashley reached down and lifted it, surprised by how light it felt. When she moved it back and forth, she felt something rolling around inside. With it sitting on her palm, she opened the middle drawer and found a pair of pencils rolling around, now so miniscule it took her a moment to even tell that's what they were. The desk was just as detailed as it was when it was normal-sized, but then again, why shouldn't it be? It was exactly the same. The only limitation now was the human eye and what it could see at such a small size.

"So there is no building of miniature furniture, is there?" said Ashley.

"No."

"So you just restore old furniture, shrink it down, then sell it out front?"

"That's exactly right," said Clara. "I love to fix old things, make them new. We tried to sell them in Salzburg a couple years ago but people didn't like them. Then I had the idea of the dollhouse shop, and dad loved it. People love buying these shrunken things."

"I can see why," said Ashley, continuing to turn over the desk in her hand, feeling its weight shift back and forth as the drawers slid in and out. "Can you change it back?"

"Of course. I can do lots of stuff with this thing," she said, holding up the shrinker.

"So my piano . . ."

". . . came from a nursing home years ago. I fixed it up, shrunk it down."

"It's all incredible," said Ashley, looking out to the main part of the store. "You've basically created a shrunken world."

"That's my goal," she said, motioning for Ashley to follow her out to the main room. "The goth house is my favorite creation." She pointed up with the shrinker as she spoke. "Forty-two rooms, all furnished with things I've restored and then shrunken down. All of it, down to the doorknobs."

"But no people," said Ashley, meaning that there were no dolls. Most specialty shops like this sold dolls or characters to show off the furniture. Clara didn't take her words as such.

"Oh, I can shrink people, too."

"What?" Ashley asked, twirling back around.

Clara held up the shrinker. "This works on people. I've used it on myself lots of times."

"You have? How? I mean, how do you get small when it's just you who operates it?" Her words were coming out fast, blurted. She could feel heat rising to her face again and she subconsciously fanned herself.

"I'll show you," she said, leading a dumbfounded Ashley back to the storeroom. Clara deposited the shrinker in a cradle on the counter which allowed the gun to be pointed in the direction where the desk had shrunk earlier. "See?" she said, backing away from her device. "I can program it to delay the beam so I can get in front of it."

"But how do you get big again?" asked Ashley, wanting to know everything about the raygun.

"I can set it to wear off. Usually I stay small for an hour. Every now and then I need fix or add something to one of my pieces of furniture." She shrugged and smiled, looking off. "I dunno, sometimes it's more fun for me to be small and work on them than make them big again. I like being little."

"What's it feel like?" Ashley asked.

Clara bit her bottom lip and fixed her friend with slightly narrowed eyes. It was so seductive that Ashley found herself looking away.

"Want to find out?"

"What?" Ashley asked. "You mean me?"

"Or both of us. It could be fun," said Clara, punching something into the touchscreen.

"I don't know," said Ashley feeling her nerve leave. "Seems really scary."

Clara nodded. "It is at first, but you'd love it. Come on," she chided. "Let's you and me have an adventure."

Something in the way she said it made Ashley's heart warm and her fear dissipate. She found herself nodding, slowly and unsurely. Clara just grinned, one of the biggest, ear-to-ear grins she'd ever seen splayed across the girl's face. She finished entering in data on the phone's screen.

Clara jogged over, took Ashley by the hand and pulled her to the center of the room, then wrapped her in a tight hug. The shorter girl smelled amazing, her hair tickling Ashley's nose. It was somewhat intoxicating. Ashley had been with more girls than boys, but leaned more toward the latter in recent years. She was feeling as though she needed to change that.

"Just relax," said Clara. "You're shaking. You need to breathe slowly while it's happening."

Ashley nodded.

Just as before, a puff of white fog shot from the barrel of the shrinker and landed upon the huddling girls. She didn't know if it was her imagination or if the fog felt cold, but a shiver ran down Ashley's spine as it enveloped them and then, just as quickly, dissipated.

"You're going to feel cold for a minute, and a little tingly, but it'll pass," Clara assured, separating. "C'mon." She took Ashley by the hand and jogged with her to the main room where they stopped abruptly in front of the large gothic dollhouse.

Just as Clara had warned, Ashley felt a ripple of goosebumps erupt along her skin. She shivered, and that's when it felt like pins and needles in her toes and fingers. Subconsciously, she balled her fists and scrunched her toes, but this affect only lasted for a moment. Either that, or she was too distracted to notice after that.

The world was slowly expanding. Her feet slid across the floor, making her reach out and grab hold of Clara who was likewise getting smaller. Both girls just stood in place, watching the room shoot out in all directions, watching the dollhouse in front of them slowly become like a real house. They were below the counter now and couldn't even see the doorway to the backroom now and still, they shrank. It wasn't until the girls were around a foot tall did Ashley realize there was a ramp on the side of the dollhouse's display that gave access to the rest of it. So Clara probably did this quite often, she thought with a snicker.

When the girls had finished shrinking, it was as though they'd entered another world. This place hardly resembled the dollhouse shop Ashley had been visiting for months. Those high shelves, the ones too far to reach even at normal size, now looked impossibly distant, as if they were starships hovering up in space. The door to the outside looked a half-mile off, and massive shapes moved by the windows. Ashley realized it was people—a whole world of giants just on the other side of the wall.

"How tiny are we?" she asked her friend.

"Six inches," said Clara. "C'mon. Let's go play."

Clara pulled her for just a moment before letting go and running off up the ramp. Ashley gave chase. The girls giggled, Ashley at the novelty of being tiny, Clara at the joy of finally being able to share it with someone. The house didn't even look like a house at this angle, right at the stoop leading into a side door. Inside, the lighting felt weird, but that was probably because the house was halved and opened like a book, letting natural light flow in through the gaping hole.

"Take your shoes off," said Clara, kicking her boots into the corner. "Feel the carpet."

Ashley followed her advice, slipping her ballet flats off and pushing them next to Clara's. The carpet felt wonderful between her toes—shaggy, almost deep. It was nearly too difficult to walk through but she managed.

"I shrunk down a roll of carpet, but not to the same scale as the rest of it. I rather like the deep, thick effect, don't you?"

"It feels amazing," said Ashley.

The rest of the room was just as fascinating. While a normal dollhouse may have looked cheap, this one was exquisitely pristine. Not only had Clara shrunken down the normal-sized items, she'd also clearly shrunken herself down with them in order to decorate. This place wasn't arranged by large hands. A tiny person set up this house.

The other rooms were just as immaculate, the carpet stretching all throughout the house until they came to the kitchen which had carefully laid tile. Ashley even stooped down to look at the grout work because it was perfect. Clara had miniaturized the tiles and the materials and had laid it just like she would in a normal-sized house. The windows looked out into the store, yet Ashley found herself continuing to climb stairs, chasing after her friend.

"Careful you don't fall over the side," she said, pointing down. Ashley's heart leapt because it looked like a hundred feet down to the linoleum floor of the shop. "But don't worry. You won't get hurt. Gravity is the same no matter what size you are. A four-foot drop is still a four-foot drop either way."

Ashley paused at each room, flabbergasted by the details. The countertops, the ceiling tiles, the working electricity when she flipped light switches, the craftsmanship of the woodwork. For a moment, she almost forgot that she was tiny, a mere six-inch woman. This place was absolutely livable, if only she had a way of getting food. Clara even assured her that the plumbing worked.

They came to a bedroom. Dominating the center of the room was a massive, four-poster bed that, like the carpet, was clearly sized up from the rest of the room. It would probably take a running start just to get on it, and that's exactly what she did. After two tries and a lot of giggles, the girls were up on the bed, feeling like the mattress was stretching out all across them. They couldn't see the floor in half of the room because the bed obscured so much. However, Ashley's eyes did linger over to the edge, near the exit to the bathroom, and found a dollhouse, impossibly small since it was smaller than her six-inch size.

"So what do you think?" asked Clara, lying back and putting her arms behind her head.

"It's a lot to take in. How often do you do this?" asked Ashley, fanning herself.

"Almost every day. Even if I'm not working. It's still fun to get to small and . . . mess around."

"How so?" Ashley asked.

Clara brought a finger up to Ashley's face, then trailed it down along her neck, around her breast through the shirt, and down to her thigh. Immediately Ashley felt warm, felt a spreading tingle course all through her body.

"You feel that?"

"Yeah."

"When you're small, you are more sensitive to touch. Orgasms are . . . amazing," said Clara.

"You have experience with this?" Ashley said coyly.

She nodded. "I do. I have a few toys I use, but never another person. I like to sleep here sometimes. It's peaceful."

"Sounds intoxicating," said Ashley. "So why am I the first? Why not bring a guy back here, shrink him down so you can fuck right here?"

"First of all, guy? Eww. No thanks. Not a fan of a dick. Second, it's hard to trust. The shrinker is a big deal. If the wrong person found out about it, it could be trouble."

"Could be a lot of money," said Ashley.

"Maybe. But probably more trouble."

Ashley blew her hair aside, then reached over and took Clara's hand. She danced her finger up the woman's arm, to which Clara met her with a smile. Before Ashley could take her time, Clara shot up, pushed Ashley back and began kissing along her neck. It was more forceful that Ashley would have guessed the girl capable of, but it was welcome nonetheless. Already she could feel herself getting wet.

Clara helped to undress her, then undressed herself, throwing their clothes into a pile somewhere off the island that was their bed. Ashley took control, swung around to be on top of her friend, then started kissing down her stomach. She could feel the tiny woman shudder, could feel stomach muscles ripple as her tongue found the sweet spot and began to kiss. Clara was moaning, her hands in Ashley's hair. Her taste and scent were overpowering and Clara threatened to squeeze Ashley's head between her thighs.

Their roles reversed and Ashley let herself go in a way she'd never before. There'd been girls in the past, but none like this. Her eyes fixed on the chandelier above them, and she realized it had once been much larger, just like everything else, including herself. Something about this whole concept was enticing, making her tremble in pure ecstasy. When she did cum, there was a lot of it, and Clara's moans become a strangled gurgle for a moment.

"Sorry, it's been awhile," she said as her friend got up on her knees and wiped her chin.

"It's fine. I rather enjoyed it. You taste like heaven." She came up, kissed Ashley on the lips and then moved to the nightstand which was a balancing act just to keep from falling off the bed. She pulled out another shrinker.

"You have another one?" Ashley nearly gasped. "How?"

"I learned how the first was made to make a second one. Then I shrank one. Not too hard."

"What are you going to do?" asked Ashley.

"I want to try something. Are you up for it?" Clara asked, finalizing data on the screen.

"I guess so."

"Good." Without giving an explanation, she turned the shrinker toward Ashley and pulled the trigger. Just like before, the white haze floated around her, and just like before her fingers and toes started to tingle. Then, it was happening again. She was shrinking, right there on the bed in front of Clara. This was a little more interesting because now she got to see what it was like to be small around a person—a living, breathing, moving, sexy person. Ashley put a hand on Clara's foot as she stood, and the giantess simply pushed her back over with her toes, laughing riotously.

"Very funny," said the shrinking woman. "How small am I going to get?"

"Relative to me, six inches. Want to go on another adventure?"

"Such as?"

Clara smiled, spread her legs and put her fingers over her pussy, resting them along her clit. "C'mon, little one. Let's have some fun."

Ashley was still shrinking when her hands found Clara's lips and parted her. She felt the large woman tense, then relax, and was slightly worried about losing a hand. But Clara's wetness and heat were inviting, so she kept pushing forward. She didn't know if it was due to her become braver or smaller, but the way inside suddenly became easy. Her face slipped past the tight wall and into darkness—but it was so hot and moist that she couldn't help but bring a hand down to finger herself.

She felt like she had no control inside the fleshy room. Wherever Clara shifted, she moved accordingly. All Ashley could do was attempt to hold on, grab handfuls of slick flesh. When Clara felt as though she were building to an orgasm, the chamber filled with her scent, and a moment later was flooded with her juices. At first Ashley thought she would be expelled but instead, Clara tightened her pussy muscles and kept the girl locked in. She was gasping for breath, and just before fear took hold of her, light flooded in, and then fingers, and she was finally resting on the warm, soft mattress again. She reached over and stroked her giantess's foot and smiled up, although it was hard to see Clara's face beyond the mounds of her breasts.

"Well that was something," Ashley said, although she was certain the bigger woman couldn't hear.

A hand scooped her up, brought her level with the largest eyes she'd ever seen. It was slightly disconcerting seeing them so close—the veins, the blood vessels, the void of darkness in the pupils. Clara blinked twice, fanning the tiny girl, and then went to work licking up the stickiness. When she was finished, Ashley felt like she could orgasm again.

"Oh my," she said. "This could be a lot of fun."

***

Sometime later she fell asleep on the pillow next to Clara's head. Ashley was a heavy sleeper, once remaining asleep during a transformer explosion just outside her house back in the states. When she woke, the first thing she saw was another eye—although this one was green, not brown like those of Clara. And this eye—was much, much bigger.

She sat up in the bed—not the same one she'd fallen asleep in—and the covers fell off her shoulders. She'd been placed here, and as the eye moved away, realization dawned on her. The store was open and there were customers inside. There were at least twenty people passing by her window. Ashley looked out across the bedroom and found where she and Clara had played, where she had fallen asleep. Now, Ashley was in the dollhouse—inside the dollhouse. These people floating by her window weren't even aware of her. There was no way they'd be able to see such a small person. A part of this turned her on.

She looked across the store and found the gargantuan shape of a woman—probably in her thirties with long red hair and a short dress. Oblivious to the tiny voyeur, she walked around the gothic dollhouse, peering into the windows, not seeing the even tinier dollhouse within it. The giantess's face was gorgeous and Ashley couldn't help but find her sweet spot and start to rub. The thrill of being so tiny, to be invisible, was so alluring that she needed to cum this instant. It didn't take long, and the woman was still in view by the time Ashley felt herself squirt between her fingers.

If she had to guess, Clara had most likely gone back to work. She didn't want to wake Ashley (which was incredibly sweet) so she simply moved the shrunken girl to the twice-shrunken dollhouse. Now, Ashley had a view of the whole store as an invisible, shrunken doll. By the time the workday was finished, her fingers were sore because she'd played with herself to the sight of every colossal giantess that happened by her window. Clara's massive body came into view, turned the sign at the door and locked it, then found her little friend in the bedroom dollhouse.

"Did you have a good day?" she said, looking to the side. It took Ashley a moment to realize she didn't want to breathe directly at the girl because the wind would probably uproot her shrunken body.

"I did!" Ashley screamed, still unsure if the giant woman heard her. Clara walked off and a few minutes later appeared in the bedroom, still much larger than Ashley but shrunken down to the size she'd been before. She scooped up her shrunken friend from the dollhouse, placed her on the floor, then grew her back to the same size, albeit still six-inches.

"You look . . .wet," said Clara, looking down at her friend's thighs. "Have fun being so small?"

Ashley's face blushed a little but Clara was there to put a hand on her cheek and give her a kiss. "It was fun alright," said Ashley at last.

"This is why I love this technology," said Clara. "We are using it the right way."

"I'd love to do this more often," she said.

"Then we will."

***

They grew to be inseparable. Ashley was learning to love her own body as much as Clara's and the things the shrinker made possible only elevated it. Ashley had a foot-fetish—something she'd been told by past lovers that it was nearly unheard of for a woman to be into, but the ability to be tiny against Clara's massive soles made her wet just to think about it.

Ashley moved in with Clara, to her quaint single bedroom apartment above, but then again, size was relative. After only a month of living there, she talked Clara into closing the gothic dollhouse, then rolling it into the backroom. They moved all of their stuff down and started living there. It was easy, convenient, and felt luxurious until they needed to get food. Then they simply went grocery shopping and made their budge go twice as far since they could shrink down to half-size and eat.

When Ashley needed to work, she just grew herself back—she'd become just as adept at using the shrinker as Clara. Then when she came home, she shrank herself with the counter-mounted device and went inside the house. This was how they lived life, and she loved every minute of it—especially on days when Ashley could sleep in while Clara ran the shop.

Clara would go for a jog on some nights, then toil late in the workshop. But Ashley would go on to bed. So Clara would shrink her friend down to six inches, pull off her own sweaty sock, then drop the shrunken woman inside before placing her in the dollhouse. Ashley loved the feeling of the fabric and the scent of her friend's sweat. It lulled her to sleep every night.

Many days she played the role of human dildo. While Clara worked in the back or even up front, Ashley allowed herself to be shrunken down and thrust inside that pussy, where she wiggled and writhed to the delight of her giantess friend. These things and more were what kept their relationship interesting and new. She never would have guessed she'd love the small town of Kurtz as much as she did, but with Clara's help, it became a second home.

One night Clara was busy working in the storeroom inventorying boxes when Ashley crept up behind her. She was holding the shrinker and she zapped the woman in the back without her knowing. But Clara had shrunken herself so many times that she could feel the change in her body before it began, and she whirled around, caught sight of Ashley holding the device, then smiled devilishly.

"What are we doing, love?" she asked. As she stood, her inches began to melt away and her head was starting to crane up to look at Ashley.

"I'm always the small one," she said. "I want a bit of role reversal tonight."

"Oh yeah?" said Clara, nearing the halfway point. "What did you have in mind?"

Ashley knelt down, let the tiny girl continue to dwindle away, then held her on her opened hand. When she finished shrinking, Ashley carried her upstairs to the now mostly cleared apartment. She pulled her jeans down with one hand just before she sat. She placed the shrunken woman on her stomach.

"I want you in me, of course. I'm a squirter, remember that."

"Oh I definitely will." The tiny woman winked, undressed, then marched straight down Ashley's stomach to the waiting pussy.